LIFE GOES ON

DOUGLAS SHELTON

AuthorHouse™
1663 Liberty Drive
Bloomington, IN 47403
www.authorhouse.com
Phone: 1 (800) 839-8640

Published by AuthorHouse 04/30/2019

ISBN: 978-1-7283-0986-6 (sc)
ISBN: 978-1-7283-0985-9 (e)

Print information available on the last page.

CONTENTS

SUIT UP

Buddy began to freak out when he realized just how serious the situation was that he was getting into. He was the next 'expendable asset' of the company to be used for this mission. Earlier in the day he had witnessed two previous divers that had not survived this mission. Both were more mature and far more experienced than he was.

He had to help with the recovery of the remains of the previous divers. He helped with the cleaning of their dry suits after their bodies had relaxed and let go of anything in them.

He struggled too much during the suiting-up process and was given a mild sedative to keep him relaxed. Although he is awake and able to perceive what happened to him, he was helpless to do anything about it.

As his close friend suited him up helping get him in the tight rubber suit, he relaxed. He thought to himself that perhaps he could succeed on this mission and his friend would not be put at risk.

He looked into the eyes of his friend one more time and noted a tear running down his friend's face.

Buddy whispered to his friend "I love you!" as the rest of the crew turned him away and lifted the heavy helmet onto his head.

One of the crew tried to encourage him by saying, "Go do a good Job boy so your friend will not have to go also!"

Buddy thought he had a great life. He recalled how he graduated and did his first open water gear dive on his 25th Birthday. The crew had chipped in and got him a birthday button to attach to his harness. He loved the diving about as much as he loved getting geared up. When he was all geared up he somehow felt larger than real life.

A couple years after he graduated, he signed up with this company and did his first Artic ice dive. Chain saws were needed to cut the hole in the ice

Douglas Shelton

large enough for the divers to enter. The lines to the air compressor as well as ropes tied to the divers would guide them back to the hole in the ice. If something happened to them they could be 'fished' out of the frigid waters.

Each dive with the company seemed to bring a new challenge. The highlight of his career was the cave dive in which they saved several scouts that were trapped in a cave when heavy rains came. The rains flooded the cave in lower spots and entrapped the scouts and their leaders. It required hauling in gear for each of the scouts. Suiting them up and giving them a basic training on the use of the gear. Individually guiding each of them thru the waters back to their waiting loved ones. It filled him with joy and pride to see each of them reunited with their families.

Some beautiful images passed thru his mind. Dives at the coral reefs. Dives into old wreckage of ships or airplanes that went down at sea.

As they secured the heavy helmet, his mind flashed back to a time when he was living in Wyoming and riding his motorcycle with a similar heavy helmet. It was when he first dreamed of becoming a diver and getting to wear all this gear. This gear that encased him in a special environment separate from the world around him. This all got started because of his love for the gear.

The sedative was beginning to wear off but he now was totally relaxed. He was now focused on the mission ahead of him. He had been briefed on the step by step processes that he had to complete. Now, he also thought he may be encapsulated in this gear for the rest of his short life and he was alright with that.

A GEAR THING

———————§———————

It all started out as a gear thing for both of us. We were both gear freaks when we first met in diving class. Buddy was very masculine and a bit of a homophobic when we first got to know each other. I don't think he feared the fact that I was openly gay as much as he feared himself being gay.

Each time I watched Buddy surface from a dive it drove me nuts. He looked awesome in the gear. He was a very beautiful boy who could make any gear look great. I about creamed my pants the first time I saw him on his Harley all geared up in thigh high black leather boots and a leather vest.

Secretly I wanted him so bad, while I thought at best, we could only be good friends. Our similar love for gear seemed to be the one thing that made the bond between us so strong. It wasn't just Biker and Scuba gear.

"Nice ass!" He complimented me when he saw me in my football gear.

We both laughed. He went on to tell how he had dreamed of playing football but he was never given the opportunity to do so. It drove him nuts when he saw pictures of me all tied up in football gear.

"That is so hot!" he commented.

To which I replied, "Dude, we gotta get you geared up!"

I pulled some of my ole football gear out of the closet and handed over to him. At first, I could see he was starting to get cold feet.

"JUST DO IT" I commented.

"Ya—Just do it before I over think it!" He commented as he let his homophobic fears fade away

Eventually, we got into Wrestling each other. I was very pleased the first time he patted my butt.

We shared an apartment and both of us loved to hang out sharing our jock straps collection. We would often watch sports with our cups bulging full while sipping on a beer and puffing on a cigar. He surprised me when he took a picture of his own shadow on the sidewalk as if it were wearing a jock strap that was laying over the shadow.

In our line of work, we often had to wear diapers to keep the dry suits clean and dry during dives that lasted for several hours. He really surprised me when he shared a deep personal secret. He actually loved to wear and properly use his diapers. He turned me onto all the variety of diapers available on the internet. While he usually was the tough masculine type, when he was in diapers, he would let the little kid inside of him come out to play and I tended to become his "daddy". Eventually, I also grew to love the feel of a heavy soggy diaper just as much as he did.

We both understood how dangerous our job could be. This mission was far worse than any other assignment we had been on. This mission had already taken a couple of our friends. As he got into the cage and they lowered it into the water I had a sinking feeling that he may not make it. I feared that I would not get that awesome feeling seeing him surface again.

RECOVERY

§

His helmet was rigged with a video camera as well as two-way communication between him and the surface. Every minute of the dive could be monitored from the surface. Crucial information could be passed back and forth between the surface and the diver. Initially, it was a comfort to me to hear his voice. He was calm now and very focused on his mission. So far things seemed to be going very well. I held onto a hope that he would make it.

A fixed camera on the equipment showed us that he had arrived at the location of the problem. Chills ran down my spine as I recalled how the first crew also reached this point. Shortly after this time was when they encountered the difficulties that eventually took their lives.

A couple of hours had passed since the start of the dive when he reported that he was about to finish but was encountering problems. His speech seemed slurred. The crew chief directed me to a task that took me away from seeing or hearing what was happening. He instructed another crew member to go with me.

The task the crew chief assigned me to was rather petty and could wait until later. I knew it was just a distraction to keep me busy somewhere away from where all the action was. I began to fear the worst. Minutes began to feel like hours. I overheard that he had stopped communicating with the surface. Something had gone terribly wrong.

I heard the crew chief yell, "git him back up NOW!"

My gut began to ache. I could no longer stay away. It seemed like an eternity as the cable slowly reeled in. It was running as fast as it could which to me was agonizingly slow.

Finally, his helmet broke the surface of the water. My usual joy of the sight faded fast as I realized his body was limp. The crew worked feverously

5

fast getting him back on board. They began to peel the gear off as fast as possible.

Someone yelled out, "He still has a pulse!"

The crew chief ordered that the Coast Guard life flight be called. He then came over to me and asked, "Would you please accompany him".

"SIR, YES SIR!" I shouted out. The crew chief was aware of our relationship. Initially, he had been rather harsh in his reactions. Now all that did not seem to matter anymore. I was going to be able to be with my Buddy.

The crew was still busy pulling off his dry suit. Warm blankets were wrapped around his limp, diapered body. Someone checked his eyes and reported they were not reactive to light. He felt very cold.

Long before anyone sighted it, we could hear the chopper in the distance. It surprised me how rapidly they had responded. They quickly got us on board and we were on our way.

The noise of the helicopter was deafening. The Coast Guard crew handed me a helmet with a headset on it. I quickly put it on and secured it properly. They could now communicate with me. They told me how long they expected the trip to the medical center would take. In the mean time they would provide life support as needed. They reported he was suffering from hypothermia. They were cautiously optimistic and provided encouragement.

I reported, "He is a tough guy—He is going to make it!!"

About that time, he opened and blinked his eyes a couple times and then slipped away again. I felt a tear rolling down my cheek. A pat on my back from the medic was appreciated. I nodded in return as I held tight to Buddy's hand.

During the long flight, I caught myself eyeballing the gear that the Coast Guard crew were wearing. The helmet I was wearing was a big turn on for me. The harnesses they wore fit snugly in their crotch. That also was a real big turn on for me. I wished that I could be wearing the same gear. I felt a tinge of guilt over getting a hard on over their gear, while my buddy's life was hanging in the balance. My quilt faded and I smiled as I thought of how turned on Buddy would also be if our roles were reversed in this situation.

A flurry of activity took place as we landed. I had anticipated this and thanked the Coast Guard crew prior to our arrival. One of the Coast Guard crew tapped on my helmet to reminded me to hand it back to them. I reluctantly took it off and surrendered it to him.

I soon got separated from Buddy. While the medical staff took care of him, I was sent with a clerk to get back ground information. She assured me he was in good hands and they would do everything humanly possible to help my buddy. I was informed they would keep him sedated to help with the recovery process.

THE REST OF THE STORY

§

His primary nurse was a black gentleman who was about the same age as both of us. He explained to me what treatments they were doing and what to expect. He also explained the visitation rules and that I could remain in the room with him and catch a nap on the sofa provided. I was about to settle in for a much-needed nap when my company cell phone rang. I had come to hate that ring tone because it meant a disaster somewhere in the world and we were going to be headed there soon.

This time the caller was the Chief Executive's secretary. She indicated that she had made arrangements to fly my friend's parents in to see him at company expense. She asked if I would be interested in picking them up at the airport and showing them around.

"Oh definitely!" I quickly replied.

She went on to provide the details of where they would be staying and the arrival time of their flight.

I have to admit, I was having mixed feelings about this after I hung up the phone. I had not met them before. I was not sure how much the parents knew about "us". I wasn't even sure if I would recognize them. I had a faded memory of seeing an old picture of them when he was a little child. It was about 4 hours before their flight was scheduled to arrive. I tried to catch a quick nap but my racing mind was not very cooperative.

Before going to the airport, I stopped by our place. I took another look at the picture of him as a little child with his parents. I then made a sign with his name on it and "PARENTS" written on it. Due to security at the airport we had to meet at the baggage claims area of the airport. I had been told the general location where the meeting was to take place. I settled into a seat and soon my head was bobbing. It wasn't long until I spotted a couple pointing at me. I recognized his mom from the picture.

We introduced ourselves to each other. I indicated that I was a crew mate and we also shared a place. As we drove away from the airport his mom ended the silence and small talk.

"What happened and how is he doing?" she asked.

I explained to her as best I could what had happened and what I had been told by the medical staff as to what to expect. While it wasn't all rosy, there was reason to be optimistic. She seemed to take a deep sigh of relief.

"He is gonna make it. He is a strong boy!" she commented.

With that a tear rolled down my cheek and she handed me a tissue.

"He means a lot to all of us!" I commented.

"Indeed!" she replied as she looked toward her husband who was sitting quietly behind me.

Their hotel was located on the route to the hospital. They agreed that it was best to check in first and drop off all of their luggage. It was midafternoon so I hoped there was a room ready for them. We explained the situation to the clerk and he got them into an available room. He arranged with the bellhops to get all the luggage to their room so we could go on to the hospital.

At the hospital I introduced them to the desk staff and to his nurse. The nurse asked if they had any questions that he could help them with. His mom replied that I had filled them in on everything and they did not want to be a distraction to the care he was providing to her son.

He replied "Good! But I will keep all of you post on any updates."

It was showing that I was exhausted and fading fast.

His mom commented "You need to get some rest!"

I asked if it would be ok with them if I went home and got some sleep in my own bed. It had been two days now without much sleep. I gave them my cell number and encouraged them to call if they need anything or if anything happened to my "Man/Boy". I squeezed his limp hand just before I left the room.

I managed to stay awake on the drive home. I dropped into my bed. It was good to be home and able to sleep in my bed. But then I thought about how empty the house seemed. I was all alone. I was too tired for my mind to go on a race for very long.

A couple hours later, I woke up with a startle. As I looked at the clock, I felt refreshed after my nap. I quickly showered and changed cloths. It was then that I realized how long I had been wearing them and how much of my "man smell" was on them. I wondered what kind of first impression that must have made with his parents.

I returned to the hospital. His mom was sitting up in a chair and his dad was sleeping on the sofa. She indicated there were no changes. I mentioned that this whole ordeal has been exhausting. She indicated that they also had not gotten any sleep since hearing the news.

"We tried to sleep on the flight up here but that was a lost cause!" She commented.

"I noticed you also called him your 'man/boy'." She commented.

"Ya!" I replied, "Most of the time with most of the people he presents himself as a very masculine strong man. Only when you get to know him well do you get to see the little boy that he still is!"

She replied "He will always be my little boy and sometimes when I really needed it, he was my strong young man also!" "He is usually not a man of many words when he calls, and God forbid that he would ever write a letter!" She went on to say. "He did write us a long letter once and it was mostly all about you! I am so glad that you are a part of his life and have brought him much joy." It is good that we finally get to see you!"

To which I replied "It is a shame that it has to be here like this!"

She nodded "Indeed!"

We agreed upon a place to go out for supper. It was getting late and not all places would be open. We decided to go out to Peggy's Restaurant out on the north side by the private aviation airport. A family owned dinner that was not spectacular but had good food.

Again, at dinner, I noted that his dad was a man of few words. I was not certain if he was just like his son in that regard or if it was a personal thing with me.

"I got this." Were his first words directed at me when the check came.

I argued "oh no you don't! I got the company credit card. This one is on them."

He nodded, smiled and patted me on the back as he handed the bill to me and commented "I cannot argue with you on that!"

Over the coming days we share a lot about our "man/boy". His mom started by sharing how she had been in an accident about the time of his first birthday. She was unable to care for him and that his dad had to fill in on the child care.

To which I commented toward his father "Picture you changing diapers."

He quickly replied, "Oh no that was not me! That was his birth father. I wasn't in the picture until he was 8 years old."

The light then came on in my head. That was why I did not recognize him from the old picture.

His mom continued on, "His father was killed in a work-related accident when he was 4 years old. What is also tough about this is that he is the same age now that his father was when he passed away."

My heart just sank as I listened.

She continued by indicating that shortly after his father had passed away, he regressed and was no longer potty trained. It seemed to be a lasting condition especially when he was put in stressful situations.

She went on to share how she met his Step Dad. His Step Dad indicated how he fell in love with both of them. He admitted that he was irritated about the potty-training issue. He truly loved this boy and wanted to see him grow up to be a good man.

He went on to explain that he coached little league football and gotten his boy to try it out.

I replied, "he told me that he never got to play football?" with a puzzled look on my face.

"Well—" his step dad replied "He was a good player but it never really worked out." The potty-training issue manifested itself out on the football field. He would either wet or mess his football gear or have to wear a diaper and get taunted by his peers. All of the taunts didn't really seem to faze him. He seemed to take it all in stride. The step father then admitted, "I was probably more embarrassed about it than he was." After one season they both gave up on football.

His step dad shared how he had a few to many one evening and came home to start and argument with his wife. At one point in the argument he called his son "a piss pants sissy" to which his wife slapped his mouth.

Their son ran away that night. They stayed up all night looking for him. They feared the worst because the temperature had fallen far below zero that night. The next morning, they spotted his breath coming out of a stack of hay bales.

"I tore into those bales." He was fine but he was chilly. He explained that he ran away because he thought he was the only thing that was stopping them from being happy together.

"I have never been drunk again since that night." The step father commented.

"He frequently taught me what it means to be a man, and he was just a child!". Most of his childhood he had been the man of the house. The step father went on to say "He persistently strived to prove to me that he was a man. I believed it! He just needed to believe it himself!"

His mom admitted, "When he had his 25th birthday I came to grips with who he was." In his life he had several friends who were girls, but never really had a true girlfriend. From time to time he would bring different girls home not sure if he was trying to convince us or trying to convince himself. After he lost his father he never stopped searching for a man in his life. He had a good relationship with his step dad, but there still seemed to be a big hole that no one could fill.

They had him evaluated by a shrink, who indicated "the potty thing" was his way of regressing back to when his father was caring for him.

"His father would change him, cradle him and cuddle him. "When he lost his dad, there was a big hole left that we could never fill" His mom reported with a tear in her eye.

I also struggled to hold the tears back as we went on to share more about my precious "man/boy". We all agreed and provided each other evidence that he was the strongest man we knew and yet was still a little boy who needed our love. I now felt I understood him and loved him even more than I had before.

THE AWAKENING

The doctor again explained that they had been keeping him sedated.

He said, "All of the signs are good now and indicate that we should cut back on the sedation."

This was the day we had been looking forward to now for what seemed to be an eternity but actually was less than a week.

A couple hours later we had no indication that there were any changes. As we were leaving for lunch, I did my usual squeeze of his hand.

"He squeezed back!!" I shouted out with joy. Of course, this canceled all our plans for lunch. We were rewarded with a steady increase in signs that he was coming around. He was moving on his own and making more noise than we had heard all week.

Throughout the week, I had been helping the nurse with his personal cares. The nurse indicated it was time for a change. His mom and dad took that as a signal for them to take a break and head to the hospital cafeteria.

The nurse pulled out a clean diaper from the closet as I started to remove the used one. With gloved hands I cleaned up the mess and got the old diaper out of the way. As he lay naked on the bed I applied some lotion and baby powder.

The nurse helped slide the new diaper under while I turned him. I secured the diaper snugly and put a big love pat on the diaper.

"I love when you do that." Were his first words and then he seemed to be out of it again.

"He spoke!" I proudly announced to his parents when they returned to the room.

"What did he have to say?" his mom asked

I thought he was out of it but he promptly replied "You don't really want to know Mom!"

He opened his eyes.

"What are you guys doing here?" He then asked but as they replied he seemed to fall back asleep.

Through the rest of the afternoon he continued to come and go.

"What am I doing here?" he asked.

As we talked about what happened I reminded him how we had lost two crewmates. I recalled the start of the dive and reminded him of how fearful he was at the time. But he could not recall anything more about the dive.

"Holy shit!! I have been here a week?" He exclaimed as it began to sink in how serious things had been.

"Oh Mom!! I am so sorry, I never wanted to put you thru something like this again!" As if he had heard us talking about his father's death. "He was the same age I am now!"

"Dad, you came too!! Buddy comment, "I am so glad to see you but I hate being such a burden to you!"

"Stop that nonsense!" His dad replied as he gave him a hug. As another tear rolled down my cheek his mom gave me a hug.

As he became more alert and oriented, we filled him in on the events of the past week. There seemed to be a lot of gaps in his memory that we helped fill in. Later in the week I heard from others how he had stood up to the crew chief and went on the dive in my place. I shared that with him and how I now considered him to be my hero. He endangered his life to save mine.

We were surprised that the company paid for his parents to come see him. That stood in conflict with our previous feeling that the company thought of us as "expendable assets". The hospital social worker indicated the company was paying for all of the medical bills and we did not have to worry about that.

Gaps in his memory continued but with the help of his Mom and dad we tried to fill them in. It was as if he had total recall of general information but did not recall simple personal information he should have known.

At a time when Buddy and I had some privacy, I confessed how I had been so turned on by the gear the Coast Guard crew members were wearing. I described it in detail so he could picture it in his mind. As I shared about my feelings of guilt, he started rubbing the bulge on the front of his diaper and laughed.

"You did exactly what I would have done." He commented.

LIFE GOES ON

—————————§—————————

The next day he was fully alert. He seemed oriented with a few gaps in his memory. The doctors expressed some concern about that, but were not very alarmed. They had him doing physical therapy now to regain all of his strength and agility. He was also working with others on his memory issues.

I told his parents that I had some other things to tend to now and that I wanted to give them some space and time with him. They both expressed gratitude for that and assured me I was welcome to stay if I liked to. I told them to call me if there was anything they need me for and tightly squeezed his hand just as I was leaving. It felt so good to get a firm squeeze in return.

I went home to clean up the house, do some laundry and just unwind. I put on a heather harness, leather jock strap and the leather collar he had given to me. That was our usual attire for chores around the house.

I also hopped on the exercise equipment for a good workout to stay in shape. I recalled how we would compete to see who could do the most on the equipment. We challenged each other as a motivation to stay in shape. We had a great program going to keep in shape and to keep fit for our challenging career.

About then, I began to miss the part of our exercise program where we would get a lot more personal, or should I say down and dirty! I was HARD, just thinking about it and I had to handle it myself.

Later, I caught up on the mail and paid off the bills that had stacked up. The hospital was already sending some bills but indicated no payment due until they went thru insurance. It shocked me how much this was all costing. But I did not worry about it because the social worker informed me it was all being taken care of by the company.

I arranged to take his parents out to dinner at a fancier place in town. They indicated that they were planning to head for home now that they knew their "man/boy" was in good hands. I blushed a little as I thought about where my hands had been earlier in the day.

They had already made arrangements with the company and the airlines for a return flight home. After a bit of small talk at supper his mom asked.

"Where do things go from here for the two of you?"

I was caught a bit off guard by her question.

I replied "I am not even sure we are an 'us' at this point. I know how I feel about him, I feel he likes me, but were not sure how this whole thing will turn out. We have just been taking life a day at a time."

I continued, "We both have to be sure we are ready for a life together and he has to be sure this is the right life for him." I went on, "He was raised with the idea that he someday would have a family and some day be a father. I don't want to take that away from him."

His mom then replied, "I know how he is very special to you and you are very special to him as well." She went on, "with the letter he wrote us and the discussion we had with him today we know how important you are in his life today." She went on, "besides, now a day's times are changing and "family" now can mean something else that includes you."

To which I replied, "But right now, we both don't know if that will last a lifetime!"

To which she responded, "No one can know anything for certain. You just hope for the best and like you said – take it a day at a time."

At this time his father chimed in, "Well I hope the two of you find a way to come see us soon. We sure would enjoy more time with the both of you and love to get to know you even better."

"Oh yes! I replied, "We both have to make sure we do that."

We made arrangement for me to drop them off at the airport on time for their flight the next day. We would first go to the hospital for them to say a final goodbye to their boy. We were met at the hospital by the medical team. They discussed what had gone on and that the next steps were to transfer him to a longer-term care facility where he would get the rehab he was needing. He embraced each of his parents as they exchanged their farewells.

About that time, I got a call from the company. In a couple of hours, I would be off on a mission. First, I bid farewell to his parents and then dropped them off at the airport.

It was a relatively simple assignment, but it was half way around the world. It felt great to be back in gear again. It was also nice to be in warmer waters and to be working with a crew that was a lot more laid back.

One of the crew mates hit on me while I was there. I very much appreciated all of his attention. But I explained the situation with my friend and he was totally understanding and supportive. We became pretty good friends while we were together. But after that assignment I no longer heard from him.

The assignment took several months and was wrapping up, when I got another call that took me back to the frigid northern waters. At least I was closer to home and able to see my buddy between diving assignments. He was beginning to regain much of his strength and agility. The gaps in his memory were less frequent.

After discussing it with the rehab team, I arranged for a little surprise for the holidays. I got some private time at the pool. After filling them in on what was happening, I also got a couple of rehab team members to help me out with a little holiday surprise.

Without letting him know ahead of time we got him too the pool. It was there that I surprised him with his present. Some new gear I got him as a holiday gift when I was in the tropics.

"What are we supposed to do with this shit!" he exclaimed when he first saw the merman suits.

"Well, the first thing we are suppose to do is get it on!" I exclaimed.

To which he burst out in laughter.

"Nice to see you got your filthy mind back!" I commented

We both got naked poolside and got the gear on. The rehab team came in handy as he still need much assistance and encouragement.

"You look like a hot catch." I complimented once he had his merman suit on.

I even needed a little help getting my suit on. Once the merman suit were on, we took to the water like a couple of fish. My suit was a little loose fitting and when I got out of the pool it slide down and showed my butt crack.

Buddy commented, "Are you trying to get something else on?"

"That is just a wardrobe malfunction." I explained, "But if you're willing and able I am game!"

The rehab crew was enjoying every minute of this.

"Soon, I hope very soon!" Buddy patted me on my bare ass.

That was my holiday present that I was hoping for. We arranged with the rehab team to let him spend the afternoon at our place.

We got to watch the New Year's bowl games at the apartment in our football gear.

"I still think you got the hottest ass in football pants!" Buddy complimented.

To which I replied, "It is great to see your cup full again!"

Over the holidays we got plenty of exercise in. It was so nice to have him there. Someone to hold and cuddle with. I thought how empty the place had felt without him there. How empty my life would be if he had not survived.

The ring tone that I dreaded so much brought our holiday time to an abrupt end. There was an urgent mission that I had to leave for in minutes. I had to hustle to get buddy back to the rehab center. For me it was back under the ice again.

WILL THE RINGING EVER STOP?

§

After the holiday's it seemed like there constantly was one call after another. I liked that I was getting a lot of travel time and seeing a lot of new interesting things. But I was also missing time with him. With all the rehab he seemed to be just as busy as me. We did miss our time together.

During one of my many calls, a crew mate introduced me to Tom of Finland. Tom was an artist in the 20th century who drew pictures about the masculine side of gay life. I guess prior to his work most people thought of the gay world as a bunch of sissies.

It was really interesting to see all of his works and to learn about the past history of the gay community. It helped me understand more about the struggle between the straights and gay community that still exists today. I even learned about a murder that took place about the time my man/boy was born in the state that he lived in. It helped me understand more about his feelings and attitudes.

At the gift shop I picked up a couple of pictures for Buddy. Also, I got a book to read more about Tom and the history of the gay community.

Buddy thought the pictures were pretty awesome. They sort of were a snap shot of our lives. He was the hot biker who somehow picked me up along the way on our journey. We decided the pictures had to go up above the head of our bed.

I got another call that sent me on a recovery dive. Retrieving bodies from the deep are my most dreaded calls. They still send a chill down my spine. But I once got a card from a family that thanked me for the work I had done and the help that it had brought to them to bring closer to this tragedy. While difficult to do, it was a job that had to be done.

This time it was a private plan that went down off the west coast of Washington. I was very saddened to hear the news that it was 4 members of a family of 5. How awful that must be for the one who remains. It also got me to thinking how fortunate I was to still have Buddy in my life.

On another call I was back in the mud or the stew as I came to call it. Poor visibility jobs were a special challenge. Often you had to be like a blind man reading brail. This time it was in a sewage lagoon. Usually I felt safe on these dives because the conditions were so awful that no creature could live it all that shit. You had to look into a microscope to see the creatures that could eat you. Those kinds of dives required a hose down and complete decontamination before I could get out of the gear.

I was more worried about the crew being exposed to that stuff. I would be fine inside my gear that would not come off until it was completely decontaminated. That process usually meant that my diaper, that protected the dry suit from me, was going to be pretty soggy and maybe even contaminated by me before this was all over.

In one of my visits with my buddy, I whined about the phone always ringing. My plight seemed petty when Buddy responded.

"I wish I could hear and ringing phone again and not hear this ringing in my head!"

He went on to explain how he may not get medical clearance to do commercial diving again. He was concerned about what he would do next for a career and even more worried that he would not be able to ever dive again. Also, the company had heard about this and made a sizable offer that he was "taking under consideration."

I had brought one of my favorite pictures of my buddy to the rehab center to keep posted on the wall of his room. It showed Buddy in his dive gear with a beautiful sunset behind him. He liked it a lot at first, but now it was kind of depressing. It seemed to be saying to him that the sun was now setting on his commercial diving career. He was worried that he would not be able to ever gear up and go down deep again.

On a much brighter note, Buddy informed me that he was getting out of the rehab center and coming home soon. He was going to be released on the first day that the sun doesn't set.

"Wow, that is less than a week away!" I said with joy.

I thought to myself I had a lot to do to make this a very special day for him. I checked with his doctor to see if he would be able to drive his cycle home.

The doctor replied, "That would be an awesome thing to boost his spirits!" They had a therapist working with him to assure his ability to ride again. They knew he was really bummed out about the dive thing and this would give him a much need lift to go with life. The rehab center provided a refresher course on riding so he could drive his cycle home from the center.

So, I went out and splurged. First, I got him a new set of leathers. I knew how much he loved leather gear. I got him the carpenter style pants that he had dreamed about getting. A new vest with three chains on each side and pockets large enough for a wallet and cell phone. Knee high boots and his old leather jacket completed his set of gear.

But to me that did not seem to be enough for such a special day. I dipped into my savings and really went all out.

Buddy eagerly got all dressed up in the leathers.

"It feels great to shed all that vanilla shit." Buddy indicated referring to the clothing he wore in the rehab center.

As he proudly walked down the hallway of the rehab center, all of the staff present and some of the other patients came to the doors and applauded him. I knew he was trying his darnedest to be a tough guy, but he had a tear roll down his cheek as he was shaking everyone's hands.

Thanks went to each of the staff members and words of encouragement went to each of the other patients. Some of them had been in the Rehab Center longer than Buddy.

"Where's my cycle?" He asked when we got outside.

I handed him the keys and pointed to his new cycle.

"You're fucking kidding me!" he said in a broken voice fighting to hold the tears back.

It was his dream bike that he had been talking about for a couple of years now.

He came over and kissed me and gave me a long embrace, while the staff and some of the patients cheered use on. Tears were now streaming down his face.

"I so don't deserve you!" He whispered in my ear.

To which I replied, "Oh hell ya you do!"

I probably would not be alive today had he not stepped in as he did. What I did for him was so small in comparison to what he had done for me. As I thought about that tears filled my eyes.

A loud cheer came from the crowd as we heard the first rumble from the engine. My Buddy was back!

I hopped onto the 'bitch seat' behind him and we were headed for home.

LIFE BEGINS AGAIN

I hopped on the back and we headed to our place to get the other cycle. We planned to spend the day cruising down to the Salty Dog where we would spend our first night back together again.

He led the way and I followed close behind from a safe distance. Half way there he turned off on a side road. I was not sure what he was up to. We parked our bikes on a paved lot that over looked the water.

I soon figured out what Buddy was up to when he took off all the leather gear and got naked down to his diaper.

He was soon out in the bay up to his butt in mud. It was good to see my little boy out playing again. This time playing like a little piggy.

He shouted out, "come on in, the mud is mighty fine!"

So, I shed all my leather gear and I also was up to my ass in mud with Buddy.

As we came out to the shore, he put a wrestle hold on me in the shallower mud. I did a quick reversal and soon had him pinned down in the mud.

He conceded victory to me and I got up. He remained laying there soaking it all up and commented,

"Man, it is great to be alive!"

Shortly after that he was getting into some more mud as it was my turn to surrender to him.

We found a small stream nearby that was great for washing up. We relaxed on the lawn for a bit and discussed where we thought we should go with our lives from here. It was the first time we shared such a discussion.

I shared how much I wanted him to be a part of my life.

He shared that he could not imagine life going on without me.

He then confided in me what he had been told about some of the events that had taken place before the accident. While I was busy with the clean up after our crew mates had passed, he had overheard the crew chief say to his assistant.

"I want to send that queer (referring to me) down next. I want to get him off my ship."

At that point he got into the crew chiefs face and said "Send me!"

A tear streamed down my face as I again realized that this had all happened to him because he was trying to save my life.

"That bastard!" I commented.

He went on to share that when the company heard about this and about how crew chief called all of us "expendable assets of the company" he had gotten fired.

There was a grand jury hearing now to determine if he could be charged criminally for his conduct.

The company was making sure that everything the insurance didn't cover would be paid for by them. When they heard he could not commercially dive any more, they offered a generous cash payment as well as training cost for any career change.

"I am going to survive this. I will be ok but, I will have to put up with you for the rest of my life!" as he broke out in laughter.

I responded, "Ah what torture life brings!" As we mounted our motorcycles he came over and gave me a kiss and then whispered in my ear and pinched my bare ass

"I think you should put a pants on." He commented, "Would hate to have road rash on those buns!"

I then asked him, "How you handling that ride of your?" As I finished getting dressed.

He replied "oh man, she purrs like a little kitten going down the highway, and when I gotta pass someone she roars like a lion in heat!!"

I laughed, "How does your head come up with stuff like that?"

A couple more hours down the road we got to the Salty Dog.

That ride wasn't even long enough for my mind to stop racing about all that he had shared. My rage for the crew chief returned with a vengeance and I thought I probably could kill him if I had the opportunity. There was no excuse for how inhumane he had treated us. If the legal system did not deal with him properly, I just may have to.

After a couple of brews, I shared how I was feeling about the crew chief with Buddy.

"You gotta let go of that shit!" Was his reply. "I had that same rage for a while and then someone showed me how it was destroying me more than doing anything to him. If you do anything to him it will just ruin your own life!"

He went on to explain that until he had met me, he had some of that similar fears and prejudice that the crew chief had.

"Look how even now all of his prejudice and hatred is ruining his life."

I could not totally understand how he could be such a forgiving person. Then again, I thought, this was still more proof that he was a truly great man.

The more I found out about him, the more I wanted to know. I have to admit that when we first met it was lust and seeing him all the different hot gear, that was drawing me to him. I still thought he was very hot, but now, I was getting to really know him, understand him and love him even more.

After having a few more drinks we were both getting a bit tipsy. We were in no shape to ride our Harleys. Some of the other guys on our crew had arranged to come down to meet up with us. They had checked into the motel earlier and I was not sure what they had in store for us when we arrived.

I called and one of them came to pick us up.

That night, we found out something about him that we never knew before. He and others had a big surprise for us at the motel.

"We're going to have a dry suit party tonight!" he cheerfully announced. "I think you are going to love it!"

We both were clueless about what he was talking about. He went on to explain how some fine restaurants have a dress code. "Well the dress code for tonight's celebration is dry suits!"

I turned to my buddy and asked "You going to be ok with something like this?"

To which he replied "Are you kidding, it will be totally awesome to be getting back into gear!"

Well the little secret that our friend had kept from us was that he was the state chairman for a BDSM organization. They had rented the convention room of our hotel and set up all kinds of kinky play gear.

First, they took buddy and stripped him down. They got a REARZ REBEL diaper on him and put me in rebel's pajamas.

I could not resist giving my little boy a big hug and a love pat on his fresh diaper.

It did not take the other guys long before they had both of us all suited up in dry suits.

Soon buddy was hanging out on Saint Anthony's cross. This was all new territory for us and we were having a blast!

I commented that who ever came up with this idea should be tied down on the spanking bench and whooped properly. Just as I said that, a person on each side grabbed a hold of me.

They brought me over to the bench and fastened me down. When I asked what was going on.

They replied, "Were just following your directions sir!". They then went on to explain how I had been the inspiration for all this.

I had told them that I want to make this a very special day for Buddy and they ran with it.

The first wallop on my ass really stung and I let out a big yelp. I was prepared for the rest of them as they all took a turn.

I could hear Buddy laugh uncontrollably as he still hung from the cross.

The next day my tosh was still very tender as we headed back toward home. There was yet one more little surprise I had in store for Buddy.

As we got close to the turn off, I race ahead into the lead and signaled for him to follow me. I turned down the road toward Hope.

Half the distance to the town I pulled off the road into the home base for a whitewater rafting company.

We got off the bikes and he comment, "OMG! I have always wanted to try this!"

I responded, "Indeed!" (the word his own mother and he often used).

The first step in the process was turning over some money to the rafting company.

We were then sent back to put on the dry suits. "Gearing up again!" Buddy commented.

It was explained to us that we would have to pass a rather rigorous test to see if we had sufficient skills to take on this challenge. After a short bus ride to the shore line where we were given a short class that explained all of the things, we could possibly encounter in our journey downstream.

The first test we had to accomplish was to swim across the stream. They were right about the strong current that would pull us down stream even here where the waters appeared to be so calm.

We let a couple other people go first to judge just what we were dealing with.

"Let's do it!" Buddy exclaimed when he was ready for it.

He wanted to go before me and I did not object. There was a team of spotters along the stream who were geared up and ready to help in case anyone needed them. We both accomplished the objective and could go on with the journey.

At first it was surprisingly peaceful as we floated along. Occasionally the quite was interrupted by our guide giving directions as well as getting a conversation going and getting us to share with each other about our lives.

The other rafters with us and the guide were rather impressed when we told them about our career. Soon we could hear the roar of the water ahead.

"Get ready!" Shouted the guide, "We are minutes away from the first rapids and first canyon!"

In the class they had explained how this first rapid was rough compared to many other rafting experiences but not nearly as bad as the last two canyons we would be going thru today.

The guide began to bark out orders to each of us as to how to row to help navigate the river. Once we bounced against the rocks and back into the current.

I was not prepared for the whiplash but Buddy grabbed ahold of me and kept me from going overboard. The trip thru these rapids was rather swift and we were soon rewarded with a reprieve.

We were instructed to paddle toward a location on the side of the stream where there seemed to be no current. The guides of all the boats were trying to keep them close enough in case we need to assist each other.

As we again slowly drifted down the stream one of the teenagers in the group started to ask us about our careers. From all of his questions, I thought to myself, this kid is going to grow up to be a gear freak. "Awesome!" Was his comment when he learned that the dry suit, he was wearing, was very similar to what we used on our dives.

It got us into the discussion about the variety of gear and how it was appropriate for various dives. We also talked about wet suits versus dry suits.

As we started to hear more noise from the river and started moving a little faster, the guide yelled out.

"Heads up were almost to the second canyon."

The guide expertly instructed us on what to do in order to get us into the proper place to get thru.

Initially, it felt like the river dropped out from under our raft. Then we slammed into the first wave and then into a second wave and still more ahead.

We finally made it thru the second canyon without loosing anyone. Again, we paused in the calm waters to regroup with the other rafts that were with us on our expedition. All of the rafts made it thru without having a man overboard.

The guide check to make sure we all were ok and congratulated us on our fine efforts that got us thru that last canyon.

There was very little time for any chatter as the sound of the last canyon faded, we began to hear another roar ahead of us.

"Ok folks, enough practice. Hear comes the big one!" The guide announced.

"Stay alert and follow my directions for this one!" He warned.

our raft filled with water going thru the first wave. Then it felt like the river fell out from under us again. We were picking up a whole lot of speed.

"Right side forward" "Left side backward!"

The guide barked out orders to keep our raft going the right way.

Just as suddenly as it had started it was all done. Soon the guide was directing us to a spot on the shore line. We headed that direction and got out of the raft. We all helped drag it on shore to prevent it from drifting downstream any further.

"Our staff will get it from here." Announced the guide.

"Yawl, can relax for a while!".

Buddy asked the guide, "Do ya mind if we get the suits a little more wet?"

To which the guide suggested where they could swim and not get into the strong current.

Buddy then directed a comment toward the young man who I thought was going to be a gear freak.

"Let's do this!!"

They both raced into the water like a couple little kids.

I commented to the boy's father, "It is great to see him be a kid again!"

The father responded "INDEED!"

MOVING RIGHT ALONG

§

Shortly after getting home, we had to get some new gear and try it out. Buddy wanted to try it on me first which I eagerly agreed to.

He surprised me by first putting a diaper on me before we both got into the football gear. I soon found out why after he got me all strapped down.

"You are staying in that until you put that diaper to proper use!" He continued on, "I am determined to unpotty train you and turn you into my little boy/slave!"

That all sounded wonderful to me. I had not used the potty in a while so the transformation did not take very long to begin.

He could tell it was happening by how much more I was fighting and squirming.

"Just relax and let it happen." He calmly instructed.

With a lingering twinge of fear, I followed his directions.

As the warm sensation began to spread, I began to understand why he liked it so much. It felt so nice and was so relaxing.

It wasn't long after that when my tummy made a big rumble. Oh no, not that too I thought to myself. "JUST DO IT!" he commanded. "let er rip!!"

I was doing it. I was quickly filling the crack in back and my balls tingled as it filled toward the front.

"Oh, that is so awesome!" I commented.

He replied, "Now you see what I meant!"

"It is so amazing that such a thing can impact the pleasure centers of my brain so much!" I continued "I think I could even bust a nut over this!"

"JUST DO IT!" he replied.

About that time my phone rang.

"Oh shit!" I yelled.

"I will get the phone and you just keep doing just that!" he commanded.
"SIR, YES SIR" I replied.

I could hear him say, "I can put ya on speaker phone!" He held it up to my head.

I had to leave again soon but there was sufficient time for us to wrap up what we were in the middle of.

As he released me from the straps, he asked

"How many times did you have to clean me when I was in the hospital?"
I lost count!" I replied.

We talked all about that while Buddy join me in the shower with all our gear on. Slowly and gently Buddy removed my gear and cleaned me up.

Back in the dive gear again for me.

This time it was with the BDSM guy who helped with the Salty Dog party.

He shared that he had a good laugh when he called and Buddy answered.

"He said you were all tied up when I called!"

"That little rat!" I replied and we both burst out in laughter. "So, I hope you both had a really fun session" He commented after he was able to stop laughing.

After we got the helmets on, I thought to myself how cool it was that we had been able to come out of our closets and we could now let a little more out with each other. Life is better when you can be real. We gave each other big hugs. But, before we went down, the Crew Chief signaled to hold on and got a picture of us together.

About a month later, Buddy began toying around with the thought of becoming a motorcycle cop. After hearing his story, the cops were supportive and even got permission from the chief to let him take a ride with one of their cycles. I could only imagine all of the red tape they had to cut to get that to happen.

I thought this would be a great fit for him. He wasn't totally sure yet. He was worried about what that may do to us if he moved to a warmer area to be on the cycle most of the year.

He also toyed with the idea of becoming a nurse like the one he met in the hospital or physical therapist like he met in rehab who helped us at Christmas. I played the devil's advocate by asking if he was romancing his care providers. He admitted that perhaps it was true but also each career had appeal to him and parts of his character that would make him a good candidate for those positions.

With the cash that the company had deposited in his account he had plenty of time to decide. He was also drawing plans to build us a new house. He wanted two master suites on each side of an open great room where the kitchen, living, dining space would be. Two bedrooms and a Jack and Jill bath would go under one the master suites. Under the other would be a private "dungeon" for us and for any friends interested in having some play time. Under the great room would be a family room and theater for game days. The garage would be large enough for all of our "toys" and even room for our pick up. Plenty of storage area for all of our GEAR. When they heard about it, the company indicated they would pick up the tab on it (but stipulated a reasonable amount that could make it all happen). Location would be the difficult part to decide.

It came as a surprise when out of the blue Buddy got a leather spider man racing suit. He then suggested that we break it in by taking a trip to the Sturgis biker rally.

"We can even stop by my mom and dads on the way there or on the way back!" he explained as he tried to talk me into the trip.

I made arrangements with work and we were on the road again.

"I have to admit, seeing that many cycles in one place at one time was impressive." I told him.

I was equally impressed with the area. I felt very much at home with all the people we met and with the landscape. I was a bit unnerved by all of the traffic at the rally.

"How do all the locals in such a remote area put up with all of crowds?" I asked his mom who replied.

"Some of them hate it, some of them like the change of pace, some of them love all the cash they bring along!"

After a little training we headed up the mountain to Sand Turn. Looking up at others excited the heck out of me. Looking down the mountain scared the crap out of me. We got all geared up for a ride of our life.

I felt a sudden tug in my crotch like someone was giving me a wedgie. To my surprise I was being lifted off the ground.

"This is fucking awesome!" I thought out loud. What a rush of adrenaline.

The steering was very similar to what I had learned while skydiving. After an hour of riding the thermos, it was time to take it in for a landing. I observed the windsocks on the ground and made the proper adjustments for a smooth landing.

There was a crowd of tourists at Sand Turn watching all of this. After Buddy also landed, we were like a couple of little boys excited about a new toy they found.

"We just gotta do that again!" Buddy exclaimed.

Several miles further down the road we met another guy in a leather spider suit at a museum. He shared that his nickname was Santa due to all of his white whiskers.

"I was about to call you that myself." I admitted.

He directed us to a nearby spot that had a collection of old John Deere farm tractors. Santa even showed us the one that he grew up with when he was a kid on the farm. He seemed like the kind of guy who would have a very interesting story to tell if you had the time to listen. I wished we would have had more time to spend with him.

WHEN LIFE GETS COMPLICATED JUST PUNT

<hr>

We were just getting back from our trip and putting the cycles away in the garage, when we got a call that would complicate the heck out of our lives.

The call was from Buddy's dad's younger brother. Even after his brother had passed away, he had stayed in close touch with the family. His uncle had called several times while he was in rehab. He was very supportive of the recovery process. His background in social work also had helped navigate some of the care issues.

After the usual greetings he asked to be put on speaker phone because he wanted both of us to hear what he was about to say.

He indicated "I got a problem here and I think you guys may be the best solution for it. Please hear me out and after that I can try to answer any questions that may come up."

"Sure!" we both replied at the same time, smiling at each other for having said the same thing. "Go ahead!" I replied.

"Well, I have a young gentleman here who is in need of someone just like you guys. At 15 years old, about six months ago, he got kick out of his home."

"Oh dear!" Buddy replied. We were both curious to hear more.

The uncle continued, "He was caught doing it with the captain of the football team. When he admitted to his parents that he was probably gay, they promptly threw him out of their home and have refused to have any further contact with him or our office."

He continued, "We initially placed him in a local foster home and that only lasted a month. We now have him in a group home. When the other kids there heard about what happened they began to torment him. The group home is being as patient as they can be but has given us notice to move as quickly as possible to find a better situation for this kid."

He then asked, "I could only think of you guys! Could you and would you be able to open your hearts for this kid?"

I burst into tears because this all sounded very similar to my own history. Before we could come up with an answer he interjected still more.

"The situation is very complicated. We need you to be in this state while he is still in foster care. If his parents continue to refuse to take him back in 6 more months the court can legally make him available for adoption and you can go anywhere, or if you like to stay here in this state, we can keep him with you in a foster care situation."

He went on, "I know this is a lot to ask both of you. Take some time to mull it over and get back to me either way by Friday."

The call ended and we both were in tears.

"We gotta talk about this one!" Buddy said. "We cannot just go on our emotions right now. We gotta think this thru and this has gotta be the right thing for all of us, especially the kid!"

I replied, "ya! He has to be the most important one in all of this! This is no longer just about us!"

We both looked deep into each other's eyes. Like a directed chorus we came up with our answer.

"JUST DO IT!"

That got both of us to laugh.

"Give me a little time before you call back so I can figure out how we can do this!" I commented

He nodded in in agreement. "SURE THING!"

Neither of us had second thought about this. We were now keenly focused on the how. I set up an appointment with the company for early the next day. I told them it was a very urgent matter. They agreed to a quick meeting.

The next day I told them about the situation and the need for us to relocate.

"I probably need to turn in a short resignation notice." I stated.

"The hell you do!" replied the CEO. "You are a very valuable asset to this company and I am going to try my dam best to keep you on board!"

He went on to explain that in the short range I could use the Family Medical Leave Act.

"After that or if you are ready to come back sooner, we will make arrangement to work with you remotely. You know we really don't need you around here. When we need you, we need you at the job site. We usually have to fly you there from here. Why can't we just fly you from there!"

My jaw dropped. It was a brilliant plan that could work.

Now I understood why they paid him the big bucks.

"I cannot thank you enough!" as I reached out my hand to shake his.

He grabbed my hand and pulled me in for a big bear hug.

"Congratulations, you are about to embark on the most important mission in your life!" he said.

"Dam right sir!" I replied with tears in my eyes.

"Let me know if there is anything else, I can help you with on this matter!" were his final words.

I shared everything that had transpired with Buddy.

"Dam! We're a go!" was his reply.

We then called his uncle back. His excitement came over the phone. After we settled him down, we asked about details of what and when we had to do anything.

They had a committee that we had to meet up with and he would set that up for next Monday. We would have to fly down to get there in time. Our room for a couple of days there would be paid for. If things went well with the committee we should here promptly and only then would we have our first meeting with "our son".

It was the first time we ever heard that expression. It brought more tears and big smiles to both of us. It still did not seem real. Was this all just a dream. We were going to be parents. Something we thought was never going to be possible. We were going to have our own family. There was just one more thing that really mattered to us.

Would our son want to be a part of our family?

A flurry of activity happened before the week ended. Some friends had heard of this and they all took us out Friday night for a celebration. We shared how we hoped that this was all not premature. Our friends assured us that this was going to happen and we were going to be great parents.

They then shared some of the more interesting times they had as parents.

I asked "Are you trying to scare us off?"

Parents of an adoptive child shared a more sobering story. They enlightened us to some of the challenges that may lay ahead. They also assured us that our love would grow strong enough to pull us thru many of the challenges.

"He is not going to be perfect and you certainly are not perfect and that is what is perfect about all of this!"

"At the end of every day, just love each other as best you can!"

We boarded the plane late on Saturday afternoon. Without any unforeseen delays, it would put us at our destination early on Sunday for a day of rest before the meeting with the committee. As usual when flying commercial we encountered some issues and arrived closer to noon. We picked up a rental car and headed to the motel.

We were on time for the committee meeting the next day. His uncle brought us in and introduced us to everyone. The small talked did not last very long. It was pointed out that we were the first openly gay couple to apply for foster care and/or adoption thru this office. They made it clear, while the law was officially on our side and they could not discriminate against us, that did not entitle anyone to get a child. Every child is entitled to have a safe and secure home to grow up in. But no one is entitled to be a parent.

We were then asked to respond to that and share why we thought we could be good parents.

Buddy replied first. "I am glad to see we are on the same page!"

"I want you to make sure we are right for our son!" I continued, "This is not at all about what is right for us, this is all about what is right for a boy who I hope will become my son!"

The next couple of questions came from the guy sitting down at the end of the table. They were all very tough question. We seemed to be giving answers that were appropriate. He then asked the hot button question.

"How do you intend to continue your passion for each other with a minor child in the house?"

Buddy responded to that one first, "I was raised in a home by a mother and father and later in life my mother and a step-father. They had no problem loving each other and taking care of me as a child. What they did in the privacy of their home when I was not there and the privacy of their room was none of my business."

I continued on, "The same was true in my family! Love between consenting adults is their business and only to be shared with other adults on a mutual trusting and accepting basis. While you as a parent may have the responsibility for teaching your child about sexuality to the best of your ability, your child should never be aware of or God forbid be involved with your sexuality. I will be there to be the parent and our son will be there to be the child. It is our duty to protect him to the best of our ability. To keep him safe and hopefully teach him how to grow up to be a responsible citizen."

The meeting went on for four hours. At which time the stern gentleman who was asking all of the toughest questions said to us, "Gentlemen, your sexual preferences go against everything that I have been taught and believe."

I brace myself for what I believed would be coming next. I heard it many times before from people who professed to be Christians but actually were just bigots. I was actually surprised by what he had to say.

"In spite of my beliefs, you have demonstrated to me the character of a good man is based on much more than just his sexuality. I was never put into a situation like you were (as he looked at Buddy). The fact that you were willing to give up your own life to save someone you love has blown away what probably has been my own prejudice. I want to thank you gentlemen for opening my eyes and opening my heart." As he continued to speak, others in the room listened intently as they wiped away the tears that were starting to flow.

"And you, as he looked at me, I can clearly see the love you have for him. I have read the records about how you were treated as a kid and the similarity to this boy's situation. Clearly you are bringing more insight, knowledge and understanding to this situation than any of us in this room have. You were right about what your friend said about being perfect. None of us are and it is all a matter of our willingness to set aside our selfish interests and love someone else enough to meet their needs. I think both of you will be great fathers for this kid!"

Buddy replied, "We were both raised just like you. We were taught to hate what we are. We were taught to be ashamed of who we are. We were never good enough. But I heard it said once by Carol Burnett, my mom tells me she was once a famous comedian, she said 'no one else can change my life for the better, only I can do that for me'! If I cannot teach anyone anything else, I hope I can teach that to my son!"

I then added, "I am glad you were asking us all the toughest questions. I wanted to go out of this room knowing that you picked us to be this boy's father, because we were the right men for this mission! Now to help you out a little in your own life, I think we both believe in the same GOD. He did not make us perfect because he did not want us to think we were him. I have my flaws and you have yours. Our GOD is an awesome GOD who is there to forgive **all** of our sins."

At which time the tough guy broke down into tears. We were the first to go over and embrace him followed by his co-workers.

As Buddy and I waited outside the room I commented, "That had to be the toughest interview we ever had!"

Buddy replied, "We are applying for the toughest job we will ever have!"

We both began to chuckle. Soon his uncle came out.

"Guys you nailed it! It was a unanimous decision!"

"Do you want to get a quick lunch and come back while I see when we can arrange for you to meet your new son?" He asked.

Buddy and I embraced each other tighter than we ever had before.

"I think we just got the toughest mission of our lives!" Buddy reported.

His uncle replied, "INDEED!"

DAD ONE DAD TWO

After lunch we got back to uncle's office. He invited us in and said he had not made any contact yet because other pressing issues also came up unexpectedly. He put use on speaker phone with the group home. They indicated our son was in school right now. We could get to the school to get him now or wait 3 hours until school was over. "getting his education is important!" I stated. "I think it is best that he stays in school and we can see him when he gets out!" The school was informed that we would be picking him up at the offices there. Uncle was familiar with them and would be with us.

We then asked if there were any suggestions on good real estate agents in the area. He then pointed out that we could locate anywhere within the state and did not have to restrict ourselves to this community. We asked what ever would be best for our son.

Uncle suggested "We may want to ask him. He may be interested in a fresh start somewhere else or he may want to stay here with his friends."

That may be the best place to start the discussion with him. Buddy planned on being the stay at home dad while I was still obligated to earn a living. Because of our mobility we could locate anywhere.

The next discussion was about the visit. We could make it just short and meet again tomorrow or he could spend the night with us in the motel. Let us also leave that up to him to decide. Either way was okay with us. If he got "cold feet" in the middle of the night we could also return him to the group home.

We went to the real estate agent and explained our situation. She was eager to get a nice commission but she was kind enough to also suggest rental options if we preferred that. We also explained that location may be uncertain until later. She gave us some books the showed and over view of the local market and what we could expect in the various price ranges. Also, any place that we got would have to meet the state foster care standards. She indicated understanding of what those issues were.

Three Thirty PM rolled up on us rather rapidly and we had to scramble to meet uncle at the principal's office. Having been shown pictures of him, it was easy to spot his red hair sitting in the principal's ante room. Uncle introduced us by our first names and then indicated we were interested in becoming his family.

"Oh wow! Two dads!" he exclaimed.

I was surprised that he had not been told about that ahead of time. I also figure this was all going rather rapidly and there had been no time to do that.

The principal arrived and offered us a private place where we could meet. Uncle explained the plans and the options that we had. Our son asked if he could skip football practice this evening to spend more time with us. The principal indicated that had already been arranged. Uncle then asked if he preferred just and afternoon and evening meeting with us or if he would like to stay the night at the motel with us.

"Awesome, I would love to stay the night with you guys." So that issue was quickly settled.

I then spoke up, "As long as we have the principal her, I would like to hear how well you do with the basic 'puppy training rules'?"

They all had a puzzled look except for Buddy who chimed in, "You know—the sit, stay, roll over, play dead, be quiet, eat your supper, do your homework—stuff like that." They initially all burst into laughter.

The boy spoke next, "I think it is going to be cool to have two dads!"

Buddy replied, "I would not be so fast on that one son! Before you had one daddy to listen too and I bet that could be a challenge some times! Now imagine it being twice as tough!" I admired buddy for laying such a good foundation with him.

I went on to say, "We will be here to love you and care for you. We are not going to be your friend. We are here to be your parents!"

He nodded his head, "I am so cool with that!" He went on to report that he thought he was a pretty good kid most of the times but some times tried to push the limits with his parents.

The principal concurred with his self-assessment. "over all he is a pretty good kid and some day he will be a good man!" The principal said.

Buddy then jokingly responded, "Darn it, that really makes it tough on us!" He looked over at me as he continued on, "you are already a good kid and we cannot screw that up!

Our son just beamed at us.

I then chimed in, "Ya, our greatest challenge is to make sure you grow up to become a man you can be proud of!"

He nodded with approval and stated "Yes sir!"

Buddy then said, "Let's blow this place now, if that is ok with everyone, and go have some fun!" Which brought a big smile back to our son's face.

I addressed to Buddy and made sure our son could hear, "I am getting to like those two words a lot, OUR SON!"

I ruffled his hair with my fingers, "Oh dad!" he replied while giving me the evil eye.

We were off to the store to get a swim suit to have some fun in the motel pool. I asked, "is there anything else that you are needing?"

"You shouldn't ask me that dad." He responded. "That is one of those places where I can stretch things a bit and get a skate board, a game system, and a TV." He continued, "But you said need dad and all the stuff I need has been taken care of by the foster home and group home that I have been in. But anything else you can spoil me with would be greatly appreciated!"

I replied, "My God I am already falling in love with this guy!"

While picking up a swim suit, we also got him a sub sandwich to hold him over to dinner later this evening. We took turns in our motel bath room changing into our swim suits. Then headed out to rough house in the water for a while.

We also took some time to relax in the hot tub and quietly get to know each other better. He indicated how he had felt closer to his mom than his dad. He felt he could never live up to his dad's expectations. Jokingly we told him how that problem is now multiplied times two. Then went on to reassure him that the only person in his life that he had to get approval from was himself.

"To be happy, you have to become the man you can love!" I stated.

We then explained our living situation and how buddy was going to be the work at home dad and I would be the runaway across the world dad.

We told him where our home currently was and he thought that was so cool because he read about that place and now wanted to go there.

We then indicated "hold on a bit" because we had to stay in this state for a while. "Would you like to stay here, or get a fresh start somewhere else?" I asked.

He asked, "I bet they had to tell ya all about my situation?"

We both nodded and stated "INDEED!"

"You are supposed to say 'jinx' when ever you do that!" he stated. We all laughed.

"Well!" he sighed deeply, "As much as I would love to run away to where you guys live now, I don't think I could love a man who runs away from his problems! Besides, with all the shit that has happened lately, I am really finding out who my true friends are and who is not."

Buddy and I both nodded our heads. "Jinx" our boy yelled and we all broke out in laughter.

I just sat there looking at him and admired what I was seeing. I then spoke, "We all have been thru some pretty tough times. We're now family and we are all going to do our best to help each other along life's journey." That brought a tear to my son's eye.

"Hey, I am hungry enough to eat a horse!" Buddy chimed in.

"Where is a good place to eat in these parts?" I asked.

"We ought to head over to the Winchester. It may take a little while getting there but it is well worth it. I have only been there a couple times because it is so expensive but it is so good!" He reported.

"We will have to promote you to restaurant critic if this place is as good as you say." I commented.

It was under a half hour drive to get there. The wait for a table was about as long. It lived up to all the promotion that our son gave it on the drive over there.

"Ya just gotta try the onion stew!" he reported as the waiter asked what we would like to drink.

"One of us is still a virgin!" Buddy reported and our son jabbed him with an elbow.

"Pants on fire!" he commented to Buddy.

"I meant drinks!" Buddy reported and the waiter just got a big smile and said, "Ya, let's just keep it PG and talk about drinks!"

As he served the drinks the waiter asked, "Are we celebrating anything special tonight?"

My son replied, "Our first family supper!"

My heart swelled with pride. I also thought to myself, this kid is pretty quick. We all placed our orders. The onion soup was awesome and the scones were to die for.

"Ya gotta get us more of those!" I told the waiter.

Free desserts at the end of the meal and we were all stuffed.

"You got the job, restaurant critic!" I reported to my son and he replied "INDEED!"

When the waiter brought the check he announced, "Kids eat first suppers free!" He went on to say, "The owner just set a new policy for adoptive families!"

"Gee thanks!" we both replied and our son chimed in, "Jinx!" Which got us all laughing again.

The Waiter then reported, "The owner would like to meet you if that is ok with you guys?"

We told the owner we thought he had a pretty awesome place to which he replied, "What is awesome is what you guys are doing for this boy!"

As we drove back to the motel, our son fell fast asleep. We discussed plans for what we would need to do for the rest of our visit. There would be some legal stuff to do with Buddy's uncle. We had to find a suitable place to live and get it all set up with utilities and even furnishings.

As we were about to exit the highway by our hotel, Buddy patted me on my thigh and said "I think we got a real winner here!"

I nodded, "Indeed!"

As we pulled up to the motel I commented, "Who gets to carry him into bed?"

"That won't be necessary!" our son replied.

I then wondered how long he had been awake and just faking it. He got to use the bathroom first and get ready for bed. Buddy second and then my turn. We were all wiped out.

NEST BUILDING

The next day we took our son along with us to find a place to live. He had permission to miss school to be with us but he did not want to miss a second football practice. We introduced him to the real estate agent and all hopped into her suburban.

"SHOT GUN!" our son yelled out as we headed to the vehicle. No one argued with him and that let me and Buddy be together in the back.

She first showed us a couple of houses by his school. It would be easy walking distances for him to and from school. They both had some short comings. The first only had one bathroom, which would be an issue when all 3 of us had to get ready at the same time. The second one seemed way to pricy for what we were getting and what we were needing.

I got one a little further out that I want to show you!" she reported. It soon dawned on me that a little way out was a lot more than I expected. Surprisingly, it did not take much time to drive there. But our son was not going to be walking to school from here.

"They have buses for school and even for extra curricular activities." She reported.

"maybe this might work out!" buddy replied. After all, he was going to be the stay home dad and have to do much of the taxi service.

It had a nice open feel to it. "Dishwasher!" buddy exclaimed. The other two places did not have that. A bedroom for each of us. Even a study for our son to do homework in. An extra room in the basement that could be our "little get away". It even had a lock on the door already. Big enough garage for the cycles but the pickup would need to stay out.

While it wasn't entirely perfect, we were all sold on it. The view of the mountains was spectacular. Our son loved it and thought his friends would also like to hang out there. It had 10 acres with lots of trees, for them to get lost in. Plenty of storage room for all of our gear. We discussed price and put in an offer. All of the appliance and much of the furnishing were included so that made it even easier.

"We gotta get back to town in time for football practice." Buddy reported. We all had lost track of time. The agent took some 'short cuts' that got back to the school in plenty of time. Our son showed us where to meet him on the practice field. He then went into the locker room to suit up. We went with the agent to finalize the offer and pick up our vehicle.

By the time we got back the team was out on the field. Now I understood why he wanted to get to practice. Today was offense vs. defense scrimmage day. I recalled how much I enjoyed that as well as the games. I was not so much into the running and calisthenics. They were good for getting and staying in shape but pretty boring. Without anything else to focus on my mind would eye the other guys and then I would feel tinges of quilt about that.

A nice football butt could always catch my eye and get my kinky mind to racing with it. I was especially vulnerable to the ones that had jock strap views.

Now that I was an adult, I made certain that was not the case with any high school or younger players. Also, now a days, most of my football gear play is off the field. I often fantasize about getting an adult fantasy team going. Some of the other kink guys at home have also talked about it. We need to just do it!

We spotted our son the center. There were a few others in the stands also watching. Some were other high school kids and some were other parents. Buddy and I seem to stand out because it was the first time any of them had seen us.

One of the other parents tried to start up a conversation by asking "Are you the recruiters?"

"You might say that." I promptly replied and buddy looked at me. "Just go with it!" I whispered in his ear.

"Who ya here to see?" Was his next question to which I replied, "We are looking for a good center!" There was no reply and an icy chill seemed to ensue. I thought to myself this is what our son is up against if he stays here.

As I watched our son I thought, dam he is a good player. Good delivery on the snap and really tough on the blocking. Any quarterback would do good to stand behind him. He was still pretty young and yet had this down pat.

I commented to buddy, "This kid is good at this and could go places with this!" meaning he was scholarship material even at this young age. He already had some pretty good size to him and the football padding brought that out even more.

As he walked off the field, I applied a butt pat and asked "Whatcha fixen for supper tonight!"

"Barbeque!" was his prompt reply.

I wondered where the heck that was at. After he got 'ungeared' he explained to us two options. The one was expensive and the other his favorite was two hours away.

"What the heck, we got plenty of time and I will be even more hungry by the time we get there!" Buddy replied. So, we were on a road trip to Dave's place.

The drive provided ample time to get to know more about each other. I started with a compliment about how good his game was. He appreciated it and thanked me for the compliment.

He then went to the delicate place that we had all been carefully avoiding. "Every time he sticks his hands on my crotch, I love it. I loved it too much to say anything about it. Besides who could I talk to about it?" He went on, "No one here would have listened to me. They all would have been quick to judge me. I wasn't even sure about myself and I was honestly even scared about it. When he did me, my doubt was all erased. I am so glad you guys are my dads so I have someone to finally talk to!"

I replied with a nod of my head, "Any time son! That is what we both are here for!"

Our son seemed to be getting comfortable with us as he continued "I am a little embarrassed to talk about this, but it seems like the gear really turns me on!"

Buddy replied, "No embarrassment needed around a couple of GEAR KINGS!"

"You're kidding!" he replied, "I kinda suspected it with the scuba and biker stuff you talked about. Oh, this is so awesome! I could not have asked for better dads."

To which I responded "We have to keep it as dads and son. We are not child molesters and not about to become ones!"

He replied, "Awesome! You guys really are my perfect dads."

As we entered the place, we could see why our son wanted to take us there. It was a large cabin structure and we were seated by the huge stone fireplace.

Buddy started the conversation, "This is how I envision our place to be! It would have huge windows on that side looking over the mountains. The fireplace would be see-thru from the living room into the dining room and kitchen. The garage back behind the kitchen and the master bedrooms on each side."

Our son chimed in, "Where is my room at?"

"In the basement, on the other side from the gear room!" Buddy replied.

"Awesome, when can we go there!" our son commented.

"Have to build it yet. But first we have to figure out where it would be right for all of us!" I said.

After we finished up the main course, I compliment, "Food critique, you are hired again!"

To which our son replied, "Oh were not done yet. You have to bring them the bread pudding, please!" He addressed the waitress. "It is just like the stuff that grandma makes!" He said.

After one bite I reported, "Yep, my grandma made the same stuff! It is really awesome."

Buddy chimed in, "shot, I hope we all don't have the same grandma!"

More laughter by all of us.

It was a good thing that I was the designated driver. My mind would be racing all the way back to the hotel. Those two were totally wiped out. Buddy even started to snore. I started thinking about all the things we had to do. Legal stuff for the adoption, getting our stuff moved to the new place and what about the long-range picture. Which way would be going and where would we end up?

At least I was sure about one thing. We had our son. We were already good dads. We were a family. We just needed to finish building our nest.

A LITTLE TENDER
A LITTLE RUFF

―――――――――― § ――――――――――

For any adoption, the state required a 'cooling off period' that had to last 72 hours. Our son had to go back to the group home for that period of time. We set a date in which we could get some of our stuff moved and drive our vehicles to the new place. The seller accepted our offer so we were moving to the place with 10 acres.

For Buddy and I, it was anything but a cooling off time! We started with a tender good night kiss and some caressing.

"Oh daddy, I want it so bad!" Were the magic words that I said.

Then Buddy was all over me! It was like he had a sudden surge of masculine power flood over him. We both felt like our nuts were going to burst in our pants before we had a chance to take them off. Buddy stuck it to me fast and ruff. He tried to make the moment last as long as possible for my enjoyment. But it wasn't long before both of our nut sacks were bursting with fresh seeds.

On the flight back home, Buddy was frequently rubbing the inside of my thigh. I had no objection to that at all. He was being discreet about it but the flight attendant did get a quick glimpse of it. He just had a big smile and offered us another drink. The thought ran thru the back of my head that we should head to the bathroom and join the mile-high club. It was too late as they were asking us to buckle up for final approach.

As soon as we got home, buddy helped me get my jacket on for some back-patio fun.

"That jacket is the only thing straight about you!" Buddy commented.

I just responded with a giggle.

To myself I wondered why we were both having this sudden surge of testosterone. I did not complain but just enjoyed every minute of it.

We even got our big toys out (the Harley's) and got some ride and play time in. There was no time for long trips but just short rides seemed to be enough to get the male hormones flowing.

After some HOT play time we would kick back and relax. Buddy would light one up and the cigar smoke would fill the room. I liked the smell of a good cigar or good pipe, but the smell of cigarettes would get me sick. Buddy was helpful and switched over to cigars.

While Buddy would puff away on his cigar, I would take some time and lick his boots. This usually got him pretty hot and bothered.

After a couple lickings, I ask "Why have we been so HOT lately?"

He replied, "I noticed that too. It may be the thought of being a daddy is going to our heads." As he pointed to the head between his legs.

"It could be that or it may be our last chance for a while." I responded, "either way I been enjoying the hell out of it!"

We both responded, "INDEED! – JINX, DOUBLE JINX!" and we busted out in laughter.

"I think that kid is already changing our lives!" I commented.

SETTLE IN

In order to get our son out of the group home as soon as possible, buddy flew down and rented a car. There was enough stuff in the 10-acre house for them to get by. I stayed behind to pack the rest of the gear we may need or wanted to have. I ran across some old leather gear that we had out grown. I thought to myself that this may be our first 'hand me downs' for our son. So, I packed them all up in a box and taped it shut with his name written on it.

I rented a trailer to haul HARLEYS and some other stuff. After I had it all packed up, I handed the keys for the house over to a friend who was going to stay in our place while we were gone. I was finally headed south. I put in 18 hour driving days to get there as quickly as possible. We had taken the route before with the Harleys on the trip to Sturgis. That trip we took our sweet ass time to enjoy all the sights along the way. This trip was about making good time and not about having a good time. It also ate up much more of that expensive Canadian gas.

After several very long days I was finally pulling up to the house. The garage door was left open and the rental car was in it. I met buddy in the garage and we were immediately in a big embrace.

"I missed you so much!" he said just as we laid a big kiss on each other.

"All leathered up?" I chuckled.

"Why not, we love it! He replied.

"Git this piece of junk out of our garage!" I referred to the rental car.

He pulled the keys from his pocket and pulled it out onto the drive. We got some other stuff out of the way and then got the Harleys in their rightful place.

"Man, that sure improved the looks of this garage!" Buddy commented. "I better go pick up our son. He should be done with practice soon." He took the rental car so our son would know what ride to look for.

I steadily worked on getting the trailer and truck unloaded and putting the stuff in the garage. We would go thru it later when we all were here and could figure out where we wanted everything. I was about half way thru when they got back. I got another big embrace after our son jumped out of the car as quickly as buddy could stop it.

"It is so good to see you again!" he commented as he lifted me off the ground with his big bear hug.

"I love you son!" was my comment, "Oh ya, I got a box here for you. Take it down to your room and check it out! It is just some old hand me down cloths that doesn't fit us anymore!"

It only took him 10 minutes to rip into the box and come back to the garage and give me one of the tightest bear hug I had gotten in ages.

"You going to model for us?" I asked.

He turned around and did his finest swagger across the garage.

"I love this stuff!" he commented. "When you said a box of old hand me down cloths, I thought it would all be 'lame vanilla shit'!" he exclaimed.

Spreading my arms out I asked, "Do we look like the kinda guys who would wear 'lame vanilla shit'?"

He shoke his head with a big smile and I got another big bear hug.

"Oh wow, you brought the Harley's." He cried out as he finally spotted them behind the stacks of boxes.

"We could not leave them behind. Like you they are part of the family!" I commented.

"OMG! There are three of them and only two of you?" he said. "Yep, we got a little story to tell ya about that." Buddy chimed in.

"Remember us telling you about the time when I was in the hospital and the first day, I got out I was given this motorcycle by your dad. Well this one here is that motorcycle. The other one over there is my old motorcycle. Do ya think you could handle another 'lame ole hand me down'?"

He was speechless or a few moments as his jaw dropped. He stared at Buddy, "You shitting me!" he said.

Both of us replied "We shit you, NOT!" "Jinx" we all yelled and laughed.

He still seemed to be in disbelief of this. We explained how it would be his to use after he was old enough to get a license to drive. He had to pass a motorcycle safety course that we already enrolled him in. He also had to maintain a high-grade average in school which we all knew was relatively easy for him to do. He would get the title signed over to him when he showed us his high school graduation certificate.

His mouth was wide open and he was speechless.

"Boy, get over there and sit on it!" Buddy commanded.

I never saw a kid move that fast before.

Buddy then instructed him how to properly mount it and to put it into neutral, pull in the clutch, turn on the switch and start it up. It came to life with a roar. Buddy showed him how to use the throttle. We could tell how much our son was really getting into this.

"This is the kill switch." and the garage was suddenly filled with silence. Don't ever play with this without one of us here to supervise you until you get your license. "One more hard rule!" Buddy went on, "These other bikes are not yours and you do not mess with them!"

I came over and put my hand on his shoulder while he sat on the bike. "There is one question I gotta ask you. How does it feel to finally have something to get excited about between your legs?"

"DAD!" he yelled as he elbowed me and we all broke out laughing.

"You want to help us with all this stuff or just sit around and enjoy yourself? Buddy asked him

"Believe me." I chimed in, "You are much better off sitting there and taking as much time as you like!"

Without getting off the bike he took a half turn and I got another bear hug.

"Don't I get any of those?" Buddy asked as he came over to also embrace our son.

Gingerboy sat there for a while longer. Like a little kid he started to purr like the motor, pretending he was driving down the highway. It warmed my heart to watch him just be a kid.

After a while he came over to us, "So what do you guys need my help with?" and he began to pitch in and help unpack the stuff for the house.

"So, what is this for?" he asked as he point to some of our 'play room' equipment. "Adults only!" I replied.

"Oh!" was his reply. As he backed away from it staring at it you could see the gears spinning in his head.

"You guys got a whole lot more stuff than I expected!" and he went on looking for more that he could help with.

I showed him how when we had packed all the stuff, we marked what room it should go into. "if you get any that says 'play room' just set them aside and we will get to them."

Try to find the kitchen and living room stuff and you can get it unpacked and put away. Let us know what it is and what you are doing with it so we can find it again. With those simple instructions he was being a lot more helpful.

"It's about your bed time young man and you got school in the morning." Buddy instructed.

"I can help some more!" He announced.

"Nope, you are pushing the limits, you know it is bed time!" Buddy repeated.

"Just do it kid!" I chimed in.

"love you dads!" Gingerboy commented and gave each of us a good night hug.

He made it as far as the leather sofa in the family room before he crashed. He had only removed the jacket and was still fully dressed in the rest of the leather gear. He had his hand over a big bulge in the front of his pants.

"I think he likes his gear!" I pointed out to buddy.

Buddy replied "Indeed! He's got his hands full there!"

MOST VALUABLE PLAYER

———————————§———————————

It wasn't long before our lives started to settle back into a routine. Buddy and I would get some much needed 'private time' while our son was at school. We would have some quality time with him on the week-ends. Every Friday night we would have a football game to watch either at the local field or somewhere at the other end of the state.

After we cheered loudly for our son when he recovered a fumble, I was noticing that we were tending to get a cold shoulder from the rest of the fans. One time as I left the concession stands another fan bumped into me and knocked the drinks out of my hands. I knew it wasn't just an accident because he softly spoke the word 'fagot' as he walked away.

People in the concession stands witnessed this and replaced my drinks for free. There were some who hated us and some who were beginning to soften and talk to us.

I taught our son, "For every asshole out there who hates, there is a multitude of angels who love."

For Halloween we had a party and invited several guests. We got 3 matching Star Wars costumes. They were ideal outfit for the gear freak in each of use. We got a real kick out of a couple of our son's straight friends. They were the tight ends on the team and they had enough balls to go out and get special jerseys that let everyone know they were the tight ends. One was number 6 with the name "tight" above the number. The other had the number 9 with "end" written above the number. That got us laughing and got our son feeling really good about his friends and himself. When they did that, I thought to myself, kids like this will teach us the way to overcome prejudice.

"I just invited the 'brave angels' that don't fear I will turn them into a faggot by having them here." Gingerboy reported.

His friends were welcome in our home anytime they were brave enough to come. They usually would camp out in sleeping bags in the family room and have a pretty fun time.

For the out of town games we would make arrangements to take our son off the bus for the trip back home. Along the way we would take in some sights and do some fun things.

Once we even went to take a dip in the mineral hot springs. We all turned into kids again and had a blast on the water slides. Our son told us about the awesome place to stay and have dinner.

"We just gotta go! Our son insisted, "After all, I am the best restaurant critic in the whole state! You even told me so!" He convincingly reported to us.

My eyes just popped out as I looked around at all the critters in the motel.

Our son reported, "There's even more to see in the restaurant and bar."

I countered, "Since when can you go into bars?"

He explained how kids were allowed in during the breakfast and lunch hours to accommodate any overflow from the restaurant. During the summer there even was an overflow patio.

"But that is a pretty boring place compared to the bar and restaurant!" our son reported.

He went on to explain the history of the place. At one time the owner of it was a big-time game hunter who traveled the world collecting trophy specimens. Not only were there animals from all over the world, there were even some creatures that I had seen before in the deep.

Talking about them helped me bridge the subject of me having to go back to work the following week. I had already discussed it with buddy and we both agreed that I needed to inform our son before it happened. It was coming down to the wire and I had to tell him this weekend.

He was very understanding about it and even joked, "Well it's about time we get you out of my hair!"

To which I responded by ruffling his hair up with my fingers again.

Something that I did frequently when I complimented him or commented on how much I had a soft spot for the 'ginger'.

This time I also rubbed the fur that he was just starting to grow on his face and commented, "Looking like you got some testosterone flowing there"

He blushed and had a sheepish grin as he looked me in the eye.

As expected, my work phone started to ring. I would be leaving shortly after dropping him off for school on Monday. It turned out to be an easy and quick assignment. I would be back by Friday, in time for the state championship game. My son's team had been undefeated all season and that meant it would be a home game. They were going up against a power house team that they had defeated once in the regular season. The other team was ready for a pay back. Our team was ready for them.

I was surprised how the local community went all out in support for the team. There were banners over main street and even the flags were put out on all the light posts. They even rolled out a red carpet to the bus of the visiting team. I was pretty impressed.

We went early, because we knew the stadium would be packed. The noise of the crowd was elevated from what took place during the regular season. Fireworks went off at the end of the playing of the national anthem.

It was on! "Game time!" I said to buddy who replied, "INDEED!"

The roar was deafening, as both teams came onto the field. These two teams were both here before. They were rivals. They were tied for the record of who had the most state championships.

The crowd even included some college recruiters who had scholarships to hand out to deserving players. Somehow, we managed to be sitting next to a couple of them. As they chatted with us, they asked if we had a player on the field. We pointed him out and told them he was the center for our team.

I also commented, "Our son is still too young to be getting what you are handing out!"

"Indeed!" the scout replied, "He is the youngest kid out there and we've been told to keep a close eye on him!"

That brought out a smile from me and a pat on the back from the recruiter. "We also heard about you guys and what you're all doing for that boy. I want to commend you for that!" he said as he reached out to shake my hand. As he did, he pulled me into and embrace and a pat on my bottom.

I comment, "Thanks, I haven't had a coach do that since I was in high school. You're making me feel young again!"

to which he broke out in laughter.

They never let out who they were really here for. When asked they replied, "There are a couple of seniors on both teams that we will be watching!"

It was a tough game. Just before half time, our team pulled ahead with a field goal. That sent them into the locker room with a real boost that would carry over to the second half. They were the receiving team at the kick off of the second half. But just as they were about to cross the goal line there starting quarterback was laying on the field.

"Oh shit! This looks serious!" commented the recruiter.

"I know that kid well. He has been over to visit a couple times!" I replied.

We could soon could see that it was a knee injury and he would be out for the rest of the game. Our son and a coach helped him to the side lines. Soon our son was back on the field. The second-string quarterback also came onto the field. He got the team over the goal line with a quick pass to one of the tight ends that we knew.

There was a fumble on the kickoff return and we were ecstatic when one of our son's friend recovered the ball and we were in good field position. It was at the end of the third quarter. If they got this goal it would be impossible for the other team to make a comeback.

Just before the snap on the next play something caught my eye. I could not believe what I was seeing. Buddy was cheering for the first down they made on that play.

I whispered into his ear, "Watch to see if you see what I am seeing?"

Buddy replied, "What the hell are you talking about!"

I calmly said, "Just focus on our son and watch closely!"

If I was wrong, I did not want to prejudice his observations.

It happened again on the very next play.

"Oh my!" Buddy shouted out just before the snap.

I was right I thought to myself. I also saw it again.

I heard the recruiter sitting next to me, "You gotta be shitting me!"

I looked into his eyes and he said, "Ya, I saw it too!"

Each time the second-string quarterback went up close for the snap, he was groping our son.

The recruiter said, "Your son is good at maintaining his pose. We need to have a good talk with both of them and determine if this is a consensual thing. Either way we need to put a stop to it."

He said he was going with us on this and we were going to talk to the coach after the game. Even though they were winning, it was painful to watch the rest of the game. I was much happier when our teams defense was on the field and my son was on the side lines. There was much hoopla when our team won the game.

"Follow me!" The recruiter instructed as he led us onto the field. We waited until all the award ceremony was completed.

He went over and put his hand on the head coaches' shoulder and said. "I hate to put an end to all this fun, but we have to get somewhere private and to have a serious conversation."

The coach then led us to a class room in the school. On our way in we could tell that they knew each other somehow. Only later would we find out that they played football on the same team in college.

Once inside the recruiter introduced us to the coach who promptly shoke our hands. "I want to thank you guys for what you are doing for your boy! He is going to be a good man soon and it is an honor to be his coach!"

As he said it, I bit my lip and a tear was in my eye.

The recruiter went on to say, "We got something more serious to deal with!" A horrified look came over coaches face and tears began to stream down his face as the recruiter filled him in on what we had seen.

The coach confirmed, "Your son came to me about it awhile back. I wasn't sure if I should believe him but I promised him I would keep an eye out for it. I even confronted the other kid and he denies anything happening. I tried to keep and eye out for it, but after confronting him I could never see anything happening."

I then chimed in, "We still gotta talk to my boy and make sure this is was not consensual. I don't want anyone to be wrongly accused!"

The coach then went to make arrangements for the other boy's parents to be called in. They would be sent to wait in a separate class room.

As the coach brought him into the room, he reported that while all the team had been raucously celebrating their victory, our boy appeared to be very subdued. He came into the room naked from the waist up, carrying the game ball. We found out later that the coach had given it to him on the way from the locker room.

When he saw us, he said, "Oh shit, you saw it!" and tears began to run down his face. I embraced him for a few moments.

I introduced him to the recruiter and indicated, "He saw it also!"

I paused, "Now son we need to hear the truth from you!"

He chimed in "Do I need to swear on the Harley manual?" His quick whit was still evident even in this situation.

I replied, "No but this is very serious and you absolutely need to be honest about this with all of us! I know this one is going to be really tough and we will still love you no matter what! But we need to know without a shadow of doubt if you in any way consented to what was happening out there!"

He took a very deep breath, "I never gave to him any permission to touch me that way and I tried my best to get him to stop it."

Buddy, the coach and I all thanked him for his reply. The coach went on to say, "I am sorry I couldn't put a stop to this any sooner, but I have one more question for you. Do you want to call in people who will prosecute this matter?"

To which our son replied, "Oh no, he really isn't a bad kid over all. I don't want to ruin his life. He's just gotta learn that he can never do this again to me or anyone else."

The coach replied, "Thanks, I really appreciate your input. But I am sorry and I cannot just take what you have to say. You still are a minor and your dads have to call this play!" as he looked at the two of use.

"Buddy, what are your thoughts?" I turned to him and asked.

He replied, "Can we have some privacy for a family discussion on this?" He no sooner completed his words than all of the others left the room.

"Man, you sure know how to clear out a room in a hurry!" our son commented when everyone was out.

I complimented him, "Kid, this has been tough and you been awesome!"

To which he replied, "You probably don't know how long and how tough it has been!"

I replied, "I am pretty sure it has been a long ordeal!"

We argued the pros and cons of various options. We came to an agreement that no mater what we decided, his fate and the outcome to all of this was in his hands and not ours. We had discussed how he had been a bully in this and our son was his victim. Our son admitted that some times he had been turned on by what he was doing to him. I explained how much of that is just the way our human bodies are wired for pleasure even if the situation may not be pleasurable.

It was good that we had talked at length about a lot of this before, on the night we drove up to the barbeque. It had laid a good foundation for our family in many ways. Our son was able to trust us and we were able to understand him as well as being able to tell when he was being truthful, which was most of the time.

We also talked about how this could all be turned into a public spectacle. Our son chimed in, "You mean a bigger one than it already has been!"

He went on to share a 'tip of the iceberg' of what that had been like. We heard him out on that and pointed out how we would be there for him as he became ready to share more about it. "But now we have to wrap this up and make a decision with your input." Buddy instructed.

We went along with our son's decision not to prosecute at this time under the condition that if it ever happened again to anyone else, we would also testify. Our son also insisted that he be given the opportunity at this time to talk with the other kid.

He explained, "I want to try to help him as much as you guys have helped me. I am not sure if I will be able to make a difference but I want to give it a shot!"

I went to the door to let the others know what decision our family had made. The other kid's family had been found and told what was going on. Everyone seemed to be sitting on pins and needle waiting to hear from us.

When the other parents heard about our decision and our son's request 'to do an intervention' they were in agreement. By this time a counselor and the school principle had joined the group. The boy entered the room dressed similar to what our boy was wearing.

He came and stood over our son and said, "You ratted me out!"

His own father quickly responded and got in his face. "I even saw what you were doing! Knock off your tough guy bully bull shit right now and listen to what all these people have to say!"

That kid then melted like a snowball on black asphalt on the 4th of July.

Our son then stood up to him as his own father sat down. "I never gave you permission to touch me that way, did I?

The other kid looked down to the floor and mumbled a reply.

Our son responded, "No body could hear you. Get enough balls to look me in my eyes and tell me! Our son demanded.

Tears began to run down the other boy's face as he lifted his head and looked our son in the eyes. "No, you never did." He replied as he hung his head and started balling uncontrollably.

I sat in shock as our son got closer and gave him a big hug. He then went on to address everyone in the room as well as the other kid. "We cannot make this about beating you up. This is about saving your life. You may not be ready to admit it yet, but you are a whole lot like me!"

Our son turned to me and said, "Dad." Acknowledging that he wanted me to give some input. I encourage him to relax and have a seat. I then started out, "Our family decided not to press charges because our son convinced us that you are not a bad kid and some day you will grow up to be a good man. You made some very wrong choices here and we want that to stop right now. If we ever hear that you are bullying someone again, we are going to be on your case like flies on shit. We all are going to be here to help you. You have to figure out who you really are and come to terms with it."

I then looked toward his parents, and continued "If you really want this to work out for the best, you are going to have to unconditionally love your son with all your hearts. Let go of your own judgements and prejudices." I briefly shared some of my history and the struggle I had with my parents. I pointed out how a choice they make can either help or make things tougher. "He still needs your guidance but most of all your love to grow up and be a man he can be proud of."

I also gave the kid a big bear hug and whispered in his ear, "Good luck kid! No matter what anyone else does, this ball is now in your court and if you want to end up being a winner, or even a survivor, it is up to you to make the choices and live with the consequences of those choices!"

Buddy then said, "You guys have said it all. I will give the kid a pass this time!" Others shared their input or offered support for all of us. Toward the end the other kids father came over and asked if he could shake our hands.

Buddy and I both responded, "You might end up with a big bear hug!" "Jinx" I heard yelled across the room from our son.

He and the other kid now looked like they had been lifelong buddies. The other kids father responded "A bear hug from the guys who are helping save my sons life would be greatly appreciated." We embraced as we were now friends playing on the same team.

The coach indicated he still had to add one more important thing. He asked both of the boys to come over. "I am glad to see you still got the game ball." He then turned to the other boy. "As quarterback I want your input on this next play. Based on his outstanding performance under pressure who do you think should be awarded the most valuable player?"

With tears streaming down his face he embraced our son, "You got this one!"

As we were about to leave, we thanked the recruiter for all his help. We explained that if it had just been us it was possible that no one would have listened to us. An outside objective reporter made this all so much easier. He indicated he had been glad to help and hoped it made a real difference in the life of those kids. He then had an interesting question.

"Would you guys mind if I keep an eye on your kid?

Some day I may just want a man with his kind of character to be a part of my team!" Buddy and I looked at each other, "INDEED! JINX" which brought some much-needed laughter.

The two boys were both directed by the coach to go hit the showers. The coach went in to provide supervision. While we were patiently waiting, the other parents came over to us and made an offer we could not turn down.

"Supper is on us! We want to take you out and celebrate your son's award!" The father indicated.

Initially Buddy and I shared with them how we felt our son had already become the most valuable player in our lives. We both thought he gave us an even better understanding of love than we had before we met him.

"Kids do that to ya." Reported his mom.

They shared how they had been heart broken when they heard about what happened to our son and his first family. We even found out that he had a brother and a sister who were left behind in his first family. It was also sad for them to witness all the prejudice in their town. They even thought prejudice may have been what drove the two boys apart.

The discussion continued on. They shared how the two boys had grown up together since pre-school. In the early years they had been the best of friends. It was only the last couple of years they seemed to be having a fight with each other. I thought after all this they actually had been life long buddies.

After the boys finished their showers and got dressed, they came out with the coach. The coach came over to both sets of parents.

"I got something else to report."

Initially, our hearts sank as we thought he was bringing yet more sad news.

Instead, he continued, "While they were in the shower, I overheard them teasing each other and laughing about who was better endowed!"

We all giggled as the mom replied, "Boys will be boys!"

SHARKS

I was just getting back from one of those trips where we had to entertain the local creatures. We were about to wrap up our mission. Initially, we had been so focused on our mission that we did not notice them gather around us. We did not want to be their lunch. We had each other's back throughout most of the dive. We stayed back to back to each other to avoid having anything sneak up behind us. I never before had seen so many freaken sharks. This felt like we were playing three-dimensional chess. Our adrenaline was pumping overtime!

Then to top It all off the flight home was very long and rough. We went thru a couple storms. Seat belts on much of the way. We were just about to land when we ran into some wind shear that tossed us about. The pilot had to abort the landing and that sent us to another airport in a remote area. The flight crew had gone beyond the time allow to legally be flying. We had to either wait until they rested or seek other alternatives. It meant I would miss my connection at the hub airport. That put me into a rental car with an 8-hour drive home.

When I walked into the house, I was already exhausted. I felt like I was walking back into the shark infested waters. I walk into the middle of a conversation that buddy was having with our son and one of his friends (The one who was the back up quarterback on the football team).

I walked in from the garage and the first thing I heard buddy say to the boys was, "You never want to fall in love with a penis or a pussy!"

Instantly I felt like I was back in the shark infested waters, I had to be on my toes to avoid be eaten alive. I quietly closed the door and sat back in the kitchen to avoid disrupting the conversation.

Buddy continued on as if he had not heard me coming in. "If you are going to spend your life with any person, you need to fall in love with the whole person and not just the part you get pleasure from!"

I quietly sat back to hear what he had to say to them.

He continued as if I was not there, "Don't box yourselves in with silly labels for what has happened to you so far at your young ages. Hopefully, you have a very long life left ahead of both of you. Give your selves time to let your lives develop and take you to the place that are right for you. When I first met your dad, I thought I was the toughest and straightest guy on the planet. I grew up with the programing that you get from parents, religion and everybody else in society. There was no way that I was suppose to fall in love with him. Most people would tell me that I wasn't even suppose to like him. Some even said I should make life for him as rough as possible. To them he was less than a human."

Buddy continued, "At first, I was afraid of becoming his friend and what that might say about who I was. I was afraid that others might think that I was also gay. I was even afraid that he would make me gay. On the other hand, I also saw the people who were prejudice and full of hate. I did not want to be one of them. That is not who I was, who I wanted to become, or who I am. That would have been so wrong for me! So somehow, I gave him a chance. I got to know what a good man he was. I ended up becoming good friends with him. That part even surprised me."

"I had no interest or intent in becoming a hero for anyone." Buddy paused for a moment, "Perhaps, especially for someone like him. But, when I heard what the crew chief's intentions were, all I could think about was him. He did not deserve to be treated that way. He had as much right to be on that boat as any of us did. He had as much right to live as any of us did."

After taking a deep breath, Buddy continued, "I did not have to think about all this. I just had to do what I did to be the man I thought I wanted to be. Before the dive, I had too much time to think about it and then I freaked out about what could happen to me. But when I looked into his eyes, I told myself 'JUST DO IT!"

"I for some reason, Somehow, let go of my own life to make sure he would have a chance at his. Since then, I let life take me to where I am supposed to be. There are times when I am really sad over what I had to give up. But other times I am so very happy with what I have been given instead. Everything in my life had to happen to bring me to this place and this time where I am right now. A place and time where I have your dad to love and I also have you guys to love."

"You can come in now!" buddy yelled out to me.

Our son jumped out of his chair yelling "Dad, you're home!" and came running to the kitchen and gave me a big bear hug.

I ruffled his hair with my fingers, "How ya doing kid?" Right then I wanted to be with buddy but I knew, our son had to come first.

"I really missed ya a lot dad!" My son commented. By now his friend was also there and he gave me a hug too.

"Good to see you again sir." Was Quarterbacks only comment.

Gingerboy commented, "Let's give them some space!" Then the two of them headed down to the family room for a video game.

As I stepped into the living room where Buddy was all I could say was "You are so fucken awesome!"

I kissed and hugged him with more passion than I had ever felt before. There was so much adrenaline rushing thru my body that I had to pick him up to carry him to his bed.

Our passion for each other lasted for most of the night. It was very early in the morning when we both passed out from exhaustion.

When we both woke up later in the day, we both asked, "What was that all about?"

I replied, "I will go first because I am sure my answer is much easier. That was all about you. What I heard you say to those boys was fucken awesome. And you, you are so fucken awesome!" I paused and we embraced again.

We then repositioned to where I was laying on my back and he was laying with his head on my chest. "Now your turn, what was that all about!"

"Oh, not much really!" he started in, "I am sure you can talk about it with them too!"

Which was a hint that he wanted me to follow up on this also.

I replied, "Talk about WHAT exactly!" I was still clueless as to what was happening.

He went on, "Oh just something simple, like they both want to be gay. They want to be happy like we are and they want to get married to each other now!"

He sensed my initial reaction to jump up out of the bed. But before I could do that, he was on top of me.

"Relax and let's think this one thru!" I did follow his advice, partly because I always enjoyed it when he was on top of me.

"I love listening to your beating heart!" he reported. I flashed back to the time on the ship when I was so happy to hear his heart was beating.

We spent another hour laying with each other tenderly cuddling and caressing. It had been a rough trip and a pretty rough night. The change of pace was very soothing. He asked about my week. I shared about all the sharks and all of the adrenaline rushes associated with that and with the flight home.

To which he replied, "Eh, sounds like you had a pretty easy week."

I replied, "Ya teenagers can be pretty overwhelming for parents. Look how we were at that age!" "INDEED!" he replied.

Our son yelled out from the kitchen, "HAY! You lazy bums get your butts out of bed. I am fixen ya some breakfast."

We had heard the pans rattling. There wasn't very much quiet when our son was around, especially with friends over. We dressed to go out and see just how big of a mess they had made of the kitchen.

"Not too bad!" I commented as I looked around the kitchen.

"Sit down!" our son barked an order at me and pointed to the place I usually sat.

"Since when did I become the pup around here?" I challenged him about barking orders at me.

"Sorry sir, would you please sit over here sir?" He corrected his tone.

I replied, "I am not upset, I am just messing with ya." As I ruffled my finger in his hair.

As I sat down his friend, Quarterback, set a plate full of food in front of me saying, "Here ya go sir!"

"Wow buddy! Whatcha been doing to these boys. This is the best service I have gotten all week! You guys did good, THANKS!"

A full plate was also set down in front of Buddy.

"Now guys sit down for a bit!" I paused for a moment as they each got into a chair.

"So, Buddy tells me you got some kind of a plan to run off to the circus or something like that!"

To which our son quickly replied, "Ah, we were actually just messing around with ya Buddy!"

Then his friend chimed in, "We were going over all we have been threw already and how much we really like each other!"

Gingerboy responded, "We also talked about how happy you guys are and how we hope for that much happiness in our lives. But we decided were not really ready for that just yet."

His friend chimed in "We still have 3 years of high school football and hopefully some college play as well!"

Gingerboy continued, "We are afraid that all of our other hopes and plans will pull us apart and end our friendship. That is why we were thinking we might be better off just getting married now. We know it isn't going to happen but we also don't want to grow apart."

His friend chimed in "We're sorry if we got ya upset! But buddy what you shared with us last night really opened our eyes."

Our son continued, "We can just take each day as it comes. If it is meant to be it will be!"

His friend added, "We will always have what we already got. Your son and I have been good buddies for much of our lives. You know we have had our ups and downs. No matter where life takes us, we will have had each other to help get us there."

"Well done gentlemen!" See you didn't really need me after all!!

They both chuckled.

"Now I got something really important to talk about! I went on, "One of you already is 16 and one of you has a birthday in 10 days. The motorcycle safety course is coming up in two weeks. I went ahead and made reservations for two!"

Both of their jaws dropped.

"You guys are going to have to talk his parents into letting him go."

Without them knowing I had already made the arrangements with his parents to do this. We just wanted to keep the boys in the practice of asking for permission for things they wanted.

"Let's go over and ask them now" my son commented as he got up from his chair.

"Not so fast boy!" I replied, "Who has to clean a kitchen up after themselves?"

"We will get right on it, sir!" They simultaneously chimed in while Buddy and I simultaneously replied "Jinx!"

"Buddy" I said to get his attention, "Harley is out there in the garage just begging to be ridden. Let's gear up! You guys can make it on your own over to his place can't ya?"

The boys replied, "yes sir, we can ride our bikes."

FUNNY FARM

I found out from our son that the place we were living in was being called the Funny Farm by many of the local residents of the small town we were living by. He went on to say that I was not so fondly nick named the 'Flaunting Fagot'.

"It is because of the way you dress" I was informed by my son who went on to point out the not so 'vanilla' aspects of my attire.

"The pants with the back door. Oh, and don't forget all the different collars and especially the heavy chain and master padlock necklaces."

I had to acknowledge to him that I was probably making a very big fashion statement in a small town.

He replied "Dad, you are just doing what you are teaching me to do, 'just be yourself'. You're being a good role model."

There is good reason to like that kid, I thought to myself. He always had a way with words and a quick wit about him. Like Churchill once said, "He could talk you into going to hell and enjoying the ride getting there."

There were some other leather men in the community besides us. They all were a lot more 'closeted' than we were. They had grown up around there and were known as the 'biker bachelors' by the locals. As if they just had not met the right women yet.

I even met a leather guy who was straight but aware of the gay community and very friendly with it. His wife was also a biker when she was not to busy raising their 3 boys. For some reason I really got to like him and respect him. We would frequently run into each other out biking. Some times we stopped at the same places and we would have a friendly conversation whenever we had the opportunity. I even found out from him that he and his wife had gotten pregnant before they got out of high school.

"Raising a family just took us down the road we are on. Who knows where we will end up once the nest is empty!" he reported.

He even had a 'bachelor cousin' who would fly out from Iowa for fishing or hunting season. To many cornfields there and not enough game back there. He traveled out with his 'roommate'. We went out fishing with them once.

In a small community like that, it felt like we were living in a fish bowl. It felt like if we sneezed the wrong way, we would have to read about it in the local press. It was even worse for our son. I noticed how other kids had many friends, while our son was very limited to just a few close friends. I asked him about it and he said he did not have any problem making friends, but often when he did the parents would not approve and restricted their kids from coming over to see him. He never got invited any where except with a few close friends.

That got us started talking about going other places once the time was up and we could officially complete the adoption. The pros of having a fresh start was very appealing to him while the cons of leaving behind very special friend weighed heavy on him. He could make new friends but never be able to replace the ones he already has.

He knew that if he wanted a good life long range, he would have to leave this place. He planned to go on to college, mostly to play football but he was too young yet to decide a career choice. After meeting us he liked the idea of becoming a diver, but we also shared about the cons of that choice.

As we went off on drives buddies old Harley was left behind in the garage. It looked so lonesome in there as we headed down the drive. All that was about to be changing. Both our son and his friend were bouncing off the walls talking about it. There excitement was contagious. We went to the DMV. They had been studying for a couple of months.

They completed all of the written exams. His friend got one question wrong but our son aced the test. They got their general learners permit and could drive now if they found any adult with insurance who was brave enough to go with them in the car or pick up.

To get the motorcycle permit they had to complete the safety course and our state would them give them a motorcycle endorsement. It was a good deal for the state. Not only did all young cycle drivers get the skills needed to reduce the number of accidents, the state could employ fewer license examiners.

All of the instructors were volunteers who were older riders who were required to pass a rigorous training program. The course also provided cycles that had been donated to the program by the major cycle companies as well as local dealerships. I thought that was a great deal as the cost of $150 for the course would be far less than the cost of fixing a Harley that went down. With our support our son's friend got his parents permission so we had two to pay for.

Buddy and I each took one with us on our Harleys. While they were busy in the two long days of training buddy and I got some good ride time (and some other play time) in. We watched the afternoon of the second day during the exam. It was easy to see how much skill they had picked up. One of the instructors told us they were surprise how serious they took this and how well they listened.

"For kids their age they seem very mature! They save their horseplay time for away from the bikes. We cannot guarantee their safety but what I see is a very positive sign!"

They both passed the exam and got their certificates. They got final instructions to take the certification to the DMV and not ride until the state issued them an official endorsement to their current license.

"Out to supper to celebrate!" Buddy announced, "Where should we go?" "Dave's place!" "JINX" They both shouted out.

PERFECT

We were out on a ride one day when we ran across one of the more interesting characters that I met in my life. He just came up to us and started a conversation when buddy and I stopped at the Steamboat rest area on one of our drives. For some reason he looked vaguely familiar.

He noticed our plates and commented, "Oh you're guys are from up north."

He went on to explain how he had made a summer long trip up there with a good friend the first summer of his retirement.

I commented, "That must have been an awesome adventure and great way to start a retirement!"

He commented that he accomplished a bucket list item of taking a dip in the arctic ocean. He was blown away that I was a diver who had often been in the Arctic. For some reason, I really got to liking this guy.

He indicated he had just completed a hike up to the top to have some time with his wife and her dog. He must have picked up on the puzzled look on our faces because there was no other vehicle around.

"Oh, they passed away years ago and their ashes are in the winds up there."

He shared how he came here often. One time as he was leaving, he had to pull over because the tears in his eyes were blinding him.

"It was then that I realized I could no longer let the tears in my eyes blind me to the road ahead of me."

It was time to go on with life. At that point buddy and I had tears in our eyes as we listened to this portion of his love story.

"Man, is there anything we can help you with?" Buddy commented as we both embraced him.

I shared with him that we were actually living in the area not to far from her.

"You gotta be shitting me!" was his reply.

It was as if he had just struck gold. Buddy and I shared about how we had to move down here for our son.

"Oh, you're the guys!" he replied.

Buddy said, "You have probably heard about us on account of the funny farm!"

He seemed to have a puzzled look as he shook his head. "No, I heard about you because I knew about your son. It is so awesome when guys like you step up to the plate and help a good kid like him out!"

I knew then that I had a new friend. I did not find out until later just how much he would mean to me. We exchanged our addresses and agreed to meet up some time soon. He even proposed a date to take us out to supper and we check our schedule and agreed that it would work out.

"Instead of out, why don't we just throw a cow on the barbee and invite him out to the Funny Farm. Buddy suggested.

So, we started to give directions and he indicated knowing the place because he often drove by it in the winter.

"You're that guy!" I exclaimed, remembering seeing him multiple times driving by on his HARLEY in the middle of winter and being jealous of him.

He showed up on time on his Harley. Gingerboy had gotten the grill ready for us. It got even more interesting when he met Gingerboy.

Our guest had not put all the pieces together before.

"SANTA!" Gingerboy yelled out, "I never thought I would see you again!"

When Gingerboy called him Santa, I then realized we had met this guy before on our trip to Sturgis. He was the guy that seemed to have a good story to tell but on our Sturgis trip we just did not have the time to listen to much of it.

"You know this guy?" I asked my son.

"Sure do! He was Santa the first Christmas I was out at the prep school.

Gingerboy explained how Santa, out of his own expense, made sure each kid at the prep school had a Christmas stoking. He got 78 Christmas stockings from the dollar store and filled each with treats for the kids.

"He was my good buddy when I was out at the prep school." Gingerboy continued "He often would bring his Harley out and take some extra time to let me sit on it! I often dreamed of becoming a motorcycle cop and he would let me sit on his Harley and pretend. He even would bring out cool pictures for me of guys on Harleys."

Our guest then directed our son, "Go get your butt back on Harley!" We all followed as our son lead the way.

Our guest said, "It has been 3 or 4 years since I last saw him! That little guy stole my heart the first time I saw that ginger on his head! When did the whiskers start?" Santa asked.

"Not very long ago!" I responded.

Our guest went on, "I cannot get over how huge he has gotten!"

"Ya, he is a big kid!" I responded.

"Can I start it up this time?" our son asked

Our guest replied "Show me a drivers license!"

Our son quickly pulled it out and proudly displayed it. I shared how he had just completed the motorcycle safety class earlier this summer and passed his test with a perfect score.

"When he wanted to be, he was a pretty smart kid" Our guest replied. "Well I guess you can start it and since you got one of these, go take it for a spin, if it is ok with your dads."

As Santa handed the driver's license back to our son who turned to me, "Oh please Sir! I have dreamt about this since I was a little kid and cannot believe it is actually going to happen!"

With that there was no way I could say no but I asked our guest "Are you sure about this? He is still a rookie on the bikes!"

"Absolutely sure. This has got to be one of those God gift things that we cannot pass up!" our guest replied.

He barely got the words out before our son was giving him a huge bear hug and lifting him off the ground. "Oh, thank you SANTA!"

"The steaks!" buddy shouted as he remembered the steaks on the grill and went running back to see if we still had something to salvage for our meal.

I instructed our son to take a short run and get back quick for supper as it probably was ready. Soon the roar of the Harley faded as he headed down the drive.

I invited our guest to head back to the patio where the grill was.

"I hope you like them well done?" Buddy comment as we got to the patio.

"Go get the other stuff out from the kitchen." Buddy instructed me.

Our guest offered to help out. "Sure thing, com'on I can use a hand!" I replied. After we got all that stuff out on the patio picnic table I commented, "What's taking that kid so long. I hoped he would be back by now!"

Our guest replied, "Oh giv'im some more time! He is out living his dream!"

I nodded my head but was still worried about my boy and my quests bike.

It was only about ten more minutes before I sighed with relief as I heard the roar of the Harley coming down the drive.

Our son came back to the patio and said "Santa, can you come with me?"

Our guest agreed and we followed him back to the Harley.

"I have to tell ya that at one of the stop signs I put the bike down!"

Our guest replied, "Oh no, are you alright?"

I could clearly see that Gingerboy was alright and I was starting to get angry at him.

Our guest probably sensed it as he put his hand on my shoulder and said, "nothing to get terribly upset over. It something that happens to all of us."

I then took a deep breath and thought back to my first time with a bike down. I could now put myself into my son's shoes.

Gingerboy pointed to a twisted foot rail and said, "Sorry Santa, but I think when I went down, I bent this!"

"HO, HO, HO. "our guest replied trying to stay in character for our son.

"That one happened one of the five times that I put Harley down! I never got it fixed thinking I would just probably do it again. I am just happy you are not hurt!"

Which showed me that 'Santa' valued my son far more than any Harley.

"Harley can get fixed or replaced pretty easy. But you are far more precious and not replicable."

With that comment I just knew I had to get to know more about this guy.

About then our son disappeared. I figured he had gone to his room to play video games. Minutes later he returned to show us a picture he had in his hand. Immediately, our guest broke out in tears when our son showed it to him.

"Damn, you still have that!" he exclaimed in a trembling voice, as our son shared the picture and commented

"That is MY Santa!"

Santa's tears were highly contagious as we all started bawling sharing the picture.

Santa ruffled my son's ginger hair just like I had often done.

"Oh fuck!" I thought to myself as I now realized how much something simple as the hair thing could have so much meaning.

While at supper, Santa shared about the 50 foster kids he and his wife had cared for. He also spoke of the adoption of four boys that everyone else had discarded.

"Tell my dad's the story about how you got the Harley!" Gingerboy chimed in.

"You even remember that?" Santa replied.

"Ya, remember you told me about it!" Gingerboy replied and went on to say. "For forty years his wife would not let him have a Harley or any bike. When she died his grandson yelled at him 'there's the Harley dealer! You can go now.' And that is how he got the same Harley he still has."

I had to admit to Buddy a few weeks later that I was really crushing on Santa. There were things about him and about his life that I admired. In some ways he was the kinda man I only hoped to be. He especially got my heart when he spoke about one of his boys who hurt some of his grandkids. He shared how he had to come to grips with it by hating the deed that had been done while still loving his son who had committed the deed. He pointed to his faith as being a guide. How God can hate sin and still love the sinner.

During the winter months I often went along with him when he took the dogs out to the ranch. It was time for the dogs to run, him to walk and time to just enjoy beauty of the world that God gave to us. I was surprised about how he shared his faith without getting all preachy like others in my life had been. He believed he had to "just do it" and not preach it or thump people over the head with a Bible. The ranch was also becoming my sanctuary. I would run up and down the hills with the dogs, while Santa would plod along the same ole trail, he always took. I told him I had to stay in shape and could not go as slow as he did. He replied that he only had to go fast enough to keep his heart going and his joints loose.

There were two spots that we always stopped at. We would hike about two miles to a spot where the river stayed open no matter how cold it got outside. The rapids were just rough enough to keep from freezing.

"Shut up and listen!" he instructed the first time we got to that spot. "let your mind hear all of this!"

Never before had I taken the time to do that. Just sit or stand there and take in nature. Actually, hear the roar of a train that was more than ten miles away. Hear the traffic on the road two miles away. Hear the birds in the trees. The howl of the coyote on a distant hill. Listen to the wind or to the quiet.

"I was too busy working to take the time to do this before!" he commented and went on, "don't wait until you are old to take time for you!" Sometimes his messages were profound.

Other times not so profound but he still astounded me with how kinky and playful his mind could be. The other spot we always went to was the Harley bench. It was a twisted ole tree where a huge old cottonwood had fallen on a smaller tree. The smaller tree was flexible and got bent over to the ground. Over the years it grew and permanently got bent into that shape. Santa saw and shared a life lesson in that ole tree.

Then I had to ask, "How come you call it the Harley bench?"

He grabbed a hold on me and showed me. He made me straddle the log and hold up my hands as if they were on handle bars. He reported that when he first came there were branches for handle bars but they were brittle and had broken off. It was a perfect height and feel.

I closed my eyes and I was sitting on that Harley.

He also shared about some other very wild and kinky things that went thru his head. He confided that his life might have been a whole lot different if he had met a "REALLY HOT GUY LIKE YOU" when he was younger. He confessed that he had a really close friend that in his words

"I could have gone gay for him!"

They really loved each other. But they both went on to meet a woman that would capture their hearts. With that he said, "let's head back to the truck. I want you to listen to something!"

It was there that he turned me onto a song by Ed Sheeran. He opened the door to the truck and cranked up the music. As the song played and he described what the lyrics meant to him.

I really listened. Those lyrics also spoke to my heart and to the one I love. Of course, all of the words did not fit perfectly for me and Buddy, I could sure pick up on the feeling. It was a PERFECT song. That even was the title of it. It could touch the hearts of anyone. It probably did as I later check out to find out what a big hit the song was back in its day. It was still pretty popular now. Santa would lend me the CD and I would listen to the album. Much of the lyrics were about everyday life experiences that we at one time or another could share. I even let our son listen to it. "Oh ya, I remember those songs" and went on to comment, "most of them are perfect people songs"

It was later that we put together a little celebration of our life together. It was on the anniversary date of the helicopter flight to the hospital. We had just a few guests over. Santa, of course had to be included. Buddy invited a gal from the recreation center over. They had become very good friends while I was off on business trips all over the globe. He son and daughter came along. They were much younger than our son who still tried his best to entertain them. The backup quarterback and his family also joined us.

Santa interrupted our meal for an announcement.

"The boys talked me into helping put together some entertainment for the evening. It's nothing perfect, but we will try our best!" he announced.

Right away as they began to play it, I recognized it was Ed Sheeran's song 'Perfect' without any of the lyrics. Our son and his friend, walked in all dressed up in my dry suits, they were doing a duet for the lyrics with just a few minor changes to personalize it for Buddy and I.

Our house was filled with standing ovations as well as many tears.

Buddy patted our son on the bottom and stated "That really was PERFECT!"

And I patted on the other side and commented "INDEED"

With the two boys in the dry suits the four of us embraced in a huge group hug that the others with us all joined in for a group hug.

CRAZY WORLD

Back on the surface I breathed a deep sigh of relief. Adrenaline was still pumping thru my body. I had never encountered anything like that before and it now was starting to freak me out. I struggled as I pulled his lifeless body. I yelled out for help from the support crew.

Some of the crew came to the water to assist me. One had a company cell phone along with him. He explained to the first responders what had taken place and was assured that help was on the way. In the mean time worked my hardest and fastest to bring him to the shore. His body was lifeless and I could not feel a pulse.

I started thinking to myself, who was this guy. He appeared to be just a kid, possibly not much older than Gingerboy. With all the adrenaline I was still pumped. I couldn't believe myself. I didn't think I could ever do anything like this. It felt so awesome to be alive, but deep down in my gut I had the thought "oh my God, how could I ever do something like that".

As soon as I got him to the shore line the support crew took over and started BLS.

When the police arrived, it really sank in that I just killed him.

"Back off and let the paramedics take care of him." The younger officer barked an order to the crew.

The paramedics continued their efforts to resuscitate. A stretcher was brought and he was removed by the ambulance.

The younger officer again barked orders, "don't touch or move anything. This may be a crime scene."

In a few moments it was confirmed over the radio for all to here that he had died and this now was a crime scene. By then the adrenaline had worn off and I just sat down on the bank and started to cry. I had just taken the life of another person and the gravity of that was already starting to weigh on me.

"Take what time ya need to compose yourself." The older officer patted me on the shoulder. "Don't go anywhere because we will need a statement from you about what happened."

I was still in my suit but the crew had helped remove the headgear. The older officer started a casual conversation asking about my personal information.

"Where ya from?"

I told him. Both my home and the company's location.

"I will stay here with ya and just let ya catch your breath."

There were other officers busy taking statements from the crew. The only thing any of them could have seen was me taking the body to the surface. Most of them indicated they first thought I had just found the body under the water. They also indicated that before now they did not think I was capable of killing anyone. I also had that belief about myself.

"How ya doing now?" The older officer asked me

"I think I am ok now!" I replied

"Before I take your statement, I have to read you your Miranda rights" He continued to recite the Miranda rights from memory.

"Do you understand your rights?"

"Yes sir!" I nodded in agreement.

"Well, go ahead and tell me what happened down there." He continued.

"We were here on a job to fix the bridge. I was to inspect some of the underwater structure. As well as a diver, I am a structural engineer. I was down there going about my business. I thought I was all alone. The guy came up behind me and I happened to turn just in time to see him lunging at me with a knife. I was able to block his knife but he did cut into my suit and nicked my air line."

I showed him the suit.

"Where is the air line he asked."

I pointed "over there with the crew"

He turned to his partner. "can ya check it out?" he asked of his partner who then complied with his request.

"What happened next?" He asked of me.

I continued on, "He kept trying to stab me several times. I would block him each time, but one time he hit me and nicked the airline. It leaked slightly but I was still receiving sufficient air. He was in a wet suit and far more agile than I was. He got close enough so I could give him a head bang with the helmet. The head bang knocked his mask loose. He backed off for a bit and got his mask back on before coming back at me and started in attacking me again. He continued attacking me and would not let up. Once he got close enough and I was able to put a bear hug around him holding his arms in to stop him from trying to stab me. We were face to face at that point and I gave him another head bang that knocked of the face mask and also knocked the mouth piece out. I continued to hold him tight. He continued to struggle. Slowly he got weaker and weaker. He released all the air from his lungs. I watched as his eyes seem to glaze over and roll up. At that point he was limp. I thought to myself that he was just a kid. I dragged him to the surface and I yelled up to the crew to get some help. I tried to resuscitate him for several minutes, but he was gone. He was limp and lifeless. I dragged him here to the bank and the crew helped me get him to where we could get off the tanks and do CPR."

"Where is the knife?" he asked

I pointed at the water, "Down there, as far as I know!"

About this time the police diving crew was arriving. The officer that took my statement indicated that he also was a police diver. I gave him a high five.

"We will see what they come up with." He said.

"This isn't going to keep me from going home?" I did not indicate our living arrangement but did indicate we just recently adopted an older boy. I did not want to be away from him for very long. I shared about my job and how I traveled.

The officer replied to try to calm my fears.

"As soon as we can confirm your side of the story, I have every reason to believe we will be releasing you soon. We will have to confirm things with the DA office before you leave our jurisdiction, our state."

My heart sank as I worried about how long this may take.

"Do ya have more work you have to do here?" The officer asked.

"Ya, I still have the supports on that side of the river to check out to determine if the existing structure is sufficient to remain in service."

To which he replied, "I hope ole Betsy won't fall on us!"

I replied "I didn't know that was her name! So far what I have found is that she is a sound ole gal."

Soon the police diving crew surfaced.

"You're not going to believe what we found! We did not find the knife but we did find a car with a large amount of cash in it."

"That explains the damage to ole Betsy's rails."

"That guy probably was a mule who ran off the bridge and was trying to retrieve the loot before his boss got his hands on him!"

The older officer turned to me. "Your crew confirmed who you are. So, we know the car isn't yours.

"I am going to release ya at this point but before you leave the state check in with us or with the DA office."

After finishing up the inspection later that week I called the officer and made arrangement to check in with the DA. The older officer from the scene met me there.

The DA reported, "you're free to go, but if we need your testimony at any point, we have you're contact information and will need to call ya back."

The DA went on to say I was totally cleared of any charges but if they ever figured out who the kid who attracted me was working for, they would also try to charge them with his death because he was still a minor.

I broke down and cried when he reported "That kid was only 17!"

The officer gave me a shoulder to cry on. He knew my own kid was just a couple years younger.

"You're going to need a lot of help with this one. Get a good professional and also talk with your friends and family. Speaking from experience, this isn't something you and stuff in your gut because it will eat ya alive."

As I was walking out, he offered me a job with them if I ever needed a job.

"Oh no, once is enough for me!" He gave me big embrace before we parted.

The company had already been notified of everything that had transpired. When I debriefed with them about the project over the phone, the CEO got on the line and indicated that everything would be taken care of by them because this happened while I was on the job. They asked if they could help me out and make the arrangements for a counselor and I gave them the go ahead.

Then they instructed me "You got a month off with full pay. Git your butt home and give Buddy and your kid a hug."

GINGER BOY

We had been using the nick name Gingerboy off and on since we first saw his Ginger hair. At Christmas while making ginger bread boys, the name Gingerboy stuck because he was snarfing the cookies down as fast as we could make them.

When March finally rolled around, we finalized the adoption. He now was our son legally and forever. We planned a big party out at the Funny Farm. I was shocked that even some friends from up north took the time to fly down for the week-end. Some of them we put up as guests in our place and some we had to put up in a local motel. We also invited the adoption judge and all the social services staff to join us. We were breaking new ground by being the first gay couple to adopt in that state. That even hit the local press.

Since it was March any celebration we had needed to be planned for indoors. We might be lucky with the weather and we might be not so lucky. We decided not to gamble and made arrangements for an indoor event.

Even Buddy's mom and step dad came over for the week-end commenting

"Hell would have to freeze over to stop them from coming!"

Those were the wrong words to say as the weather turned nasty the Friday before the party. Fortunately, they had already arrived before the weather front had moved in. They stay in one of the guest rooms in our house so they could have more quality time with their new grandson. The even arrived early enough to join us at the courthouse for the legal process. Buddy's uncle was also there.

Buddy and I got a huge portrait that covered the whole wall of the living room. It was his favorite picture as the center of the football team. This week-end he was going to be the center of attention.

Jokingly, his friends turned the event into a baby shower. He got a few nice gifts but mostly he got things that a baby would use. Binkie, blankie, bottle, and teddy bear. Even a cookie monster outfit with his size diaper and a stuffed cookie monster. I wondered what was wrong when he ran off from the party for a while. He was such a good sport that he put on his new outfit, even the diaper. Buddy and I split a gut laughing when we first saw him as did everyone else in the house.

Grandma yelled out, "I gotta get my first baby picture to show the folks back home."

Our boy had to make several poses for her which got everyone laughing even more.

Toward the end of the party he indicated he had something to say. We got everyone's attention to quiet down.

"You really didn't need to do all this. I don't really need this!" He commented as he tugged on his diaper which got us all laughing again.

someone argued "Oh yes you do!" which got him to break out laughing as he commented "You know me too well!"

Then he motioned for quiet again, "seriously, something else needs to be said!"

As quiet rolled over the room he motioned us and commanded "Dads, I need your over here!"

Buddy replied "You need a change already?" which broke everybody into laughter again.

Our son could not help himself from doubling over laughing.

He could not be out done so he replied "Hell no but if you keep making me laugh like this You will have to change me!"

Which got everybody going again. Grandma was laughing so hard she had tears rolling down her face. Buddy whispered in my ear "It is so good to see her laugh again!"

Eventually, thing settled and he started to speak. "First, we all want to thank everyone for coming tonight and making this special time even more special. Especially you, Grandma and grandpa!"

To which Grandma replied, "It is great to finally be called that. Isn't it!"

And she nudged her husband who replied,

"Naw, yawl are just making me feel older!"

Which brought more laughter.

"We should start a comedy club here!" our son replied.

He continued after the laugher quieted. "I didn't need any of this tonight! As tears started filling his eyes. Everybody got sullen and wondered what was wrong.

He went on in a broken voice looking at us, "All I ever really needed in my life is the love and understanding these two guys have given to me!"

Streams of tears flowed from everyone's eyes as the three of us embraced each other. I thought to myself, how did I get so damn lucky to get these people in my life.

By June of the summer before his sophomore year we had to make a decision on what we were going to do. By then our little Gingerboy was already a pretty big man. We had to make a choice before football practice started in mid-August. If we were going to move up north again, we could not wait until football was over. We all weighed the pros and the cons of such a move and discussed at length what the impact may be on each of our lives. Both Buddy and I had been thru this before and knew what to expect. But it seemed a lot tougher this time now that we had a family.

Our friend had been leasing and house sitting our place up north. He was about to make a move and the place would be empty in May. It was time to decide. We also discussed plans to make our dream home up north. If we wanted to do that, we would have to start that in the summer also. The house in town would just be a temporary stop over until the place was completed.

For Gingerboy, it would be the one of toughest decision he had to make in his life so far. He carefully weighed the pros and cons. We seemed to be hearing more of the cons as he would be missing his friends. Because of the graduation of the quarter back his friend was now going to be first string quarterback. That seemed to be the heaviest thing he was thinking about. By now, Buddy and I were pretty much sold on the move back north. But if Gingerboy was not with us on this and included in the decision it wasn't going to work. He knew what we were thinking and he also knew he had some bargaining power in this situation. We wondered what he would do with it.

"Okay! I got a proposal for you guys!" He announced when he got back from school one evening. My friend (Quarterback) has gotten permission from his parents to go along with us up north for just the summer. If he doesn't come along, I will be all by myself for the summer. When football starts, he can fly back. I can also make some new friends on the new football team and once school starts. Besides that, he has never been there before and this is his best chance to get a taste of what is out there in this world. Perhaps that will be enough so he won't feel he is trapped here also.

Buddy looked me in the eye and nodded his approval. I spoke, "That really sounds like and awesome plan!"

Gingerboy gave two thumbs up and said, "Yes! We got a deal. Let's just do this!"

THE BIGGEST DICK

At first, the changes were all very subtle. I found myself to be taking charge of the situation we were in much more. From there it moved on to 'you better do it my way or hit the highway'. One day I got upset with one of the support crew and I shouted at him, "Your fired!" Even though I did not have the authority to do that, they did reassign the guy somewhere else away from me!" That's is all that mattered to me, it seemed.

At first, I did not think to much about it. I was too busy going on with life. We had our big anniversary celebration. We were busy getting ready to make the big move north. My Gingerboy talked me into coming along to the M&M center and even got me geared up and out on the ice. For me that was a fantasy come true.

Gingerboy said it best, "Why don't you just join one of the hockey teams yourself instead of just living vicariously thru me!"

Between work, practice, matches, time with Gingerboy and Buddy, as well as a generally busy life there was no time left for the counseling session and I terminated them.

Initially, I thought the counselor was a rookie and did not know much about life. Then I thought he was just a pervert when he started to ask to many questions about my lifestyle. Besides, I did not need him. I was doing just fine! So, I thought.

My night life was taking a little bit of a change also. With the team and other people, I had met from biking I was spending less and less time with my Buddy and more and more time at a place called 'buddies bar'.

Even in the bar I was changing. It used to be one or two were enough to last me the whole evening. Now it seemed like I could drink any challengers under the bar. Oh ya, and you better not give me any shit. I used to be meek and mild and take other peoples shit and ignore it or turn it into fertilizer. Now I was back at them and smearing the shit in their faces.

I had enough sense about me to not drink and drive or my friends were really good about getting my keys and getting me home. Sometimes I even called my Gingerboy to be my taxi. A couple times we exchanged heated words. In actuality it really was just a stupid drunk getting into an argument with a very smart kid. In one of our arguments, I got so pissed at him that I nailed him to the wall and yelled in his face. I could not sleep that night because I hated myself so much for doing that. Somehow, I still admired him thru all of it and tried not to blame him for what was going on with me.

Buddy may have been taking the brunt of all this. The tenderness was gone. I was getting rough with him not only in the bedroom but in every aspect of our life. I stopped treating him like he was still my super hero. I stopped loving him and started owning him. It really freaked me out one night when I woke up catching myself trying to strangle him. After that I was scared and moved away to the other bedroom. It felt like we were falling apart.

Buddy was spending more and more time with his lady friend from the exercise center. They either were working out at the center or they were working out in our bedroom. One time, when I came home after having a few too many, I snapped at her,

"Are you getting banged enough?"

She slapped my mouth. I looked at her with a glare,

"Don't you dare to ever do that again!" I said in a very threatening way.

At that point, Buddy stood between me and her to protect her. He just stared me down.

"Fine, go bang your bitch some more!" I went to the fridge to grab more brew and headed out to the patio.

A couple days later I got a call from Santa. He wanted to invite me to go out to the ranch with him again.

"You are going to be leaving soon and I love to spend some time with ya!" was his invitation.

I hesitated to go indicating I was pretty busy with getting ready to move. I had him on speaker phone and Buddy was there to chime in,

"Go ahead, I got this here!"

I found out later that Buddy had set this all up. He told Santa about the tip of the iceberg that he was seeing. There was something going on. There was something different about me. Santa agreed to spend some time with me and try to figure out what was up with me.

We rode out to the ranch together in his truck with Toby and Cedar (his two dogs). They were pretty good companions that would run up and down the hills while Santa took his sweet ass time on his stroll.

At the Harley tree I sat down and straddling the tree and pretending it was a Harley. Santa came and sat down behind me. Putting his arms around me he gave me a big hug.

"I am really going to miss the times we shared here!" he whispered in my ear.

Somehow, he had a magical way of stealing my heart. "Ya! You been a great Papa for me!"

He had often talked about his kids and grandkids. They were so very special to him. At Christmas, he had shown me the stockings that he had made for all of his kids and grandkids. He was a big supporter of adoptions and had adopted four boys. He had confided in me that shortly after Christmas he had started making a stocking for Gingerboy. This was probably going to be the last time I got out to the ranch with him. He was a good ole fart and I was going to miss him a lot.

But our time with each other wasn't over. I was pretty sure he had heard about the way I had been acting lately. He had the keys to the truck and we were not going anywhere until I heard him out.

He surprised me when he started in, "How have you been!"

to which I started going on about how busy I was and how fucked up every thing was in the whole world.

He stopped me "Boy, you sure are in a rough place! We both know that you don't have the power to change the whole world. We can barely manage our own life." From his comments I know what was wrong and that I really needed to get back in focus.

He went on to say, "I see you have even made a wardrobe change. You always were more of a back door kinda guy and now you got a front door!" He pointed out the change in the kind of pants that I was wearing.

What else has been happening?" He paused to let me think for a moment.

I thought out loud, "Oh God! Give me the strength for this?"

I paused for a moment, "Am I even ready for this?"

I then broke down bawling uncontrollably as I leaned back into his body letting his arms wrap around me.

- "I killed a kid!

As the bawling got even worse. He just held me even tighter.

"Take your time and let it all out kid." Were his instructions to me.

The bawling continued as I spoke "I hate myself and I hate what I have become!"

With a few more tears I blurted out, "Some days I think it would have been better if I had just let him kill me. I don't like who I have become and I don't want to go on any more like this."

Santa started to speak, "I am very glad you are alive!"

He held me ever tighter. "I love you and you have a whole lot of others out there, who know you better than me and who love you even more than me!"

He held me tight and started to slightly rock me from sided to side. I hadn't felt like this since I was a little baby cradled in my parents' arms. I felt so helpless and needed someone so much to trust.

Santa went on to say, "Now is as good a time as any, to stop beating yourself up."

I began leaning into him as much as I dared to without knocking him over.

"You are a good kid, a good man." He continued on. "You've gotten off on this dirt road, and we gotta help pull ya out of the mire and getcha back on the right highway!"

"Are you ready to now?" he asked after I stopped bawling.

My reply surprised me, "Can ya just hold me a while longer dad?"

He squeezed me as tight as he could as long as he could. I cried as I thought back to when my dad and mom kicked me out of their lives. When I told them about who I was, all I needed from them was to held a lot tighter for a little longer.

As we walked back to the truck, I placed my hand in Santa's hand. "I want to thank you man for being here for me!" I commented.

After a few more steps he replied "I only tried to do what Jesus would do!"

After letting that really sink in, I replied, "I got some bridges to build with him too!"

As we got to the truck Santa again asked, "You got a whole lot more bridges to build. Are you ready to start?"

"Indeed!" I replied.

He then asked me to get the dogs in and said, "I need to make a quick call!" As he walked away a short distance saying "I hope we have signal here!" He apparently got through to the person he was calling. I overheard him say, "It's time, I will be there in about 30 minutes." I began to worry that I had delayed him or kept him from somewhere else that he had to be.

We stopped at his place first to drop off the dogs and feed them. I was puzzled as to why we were doing that first but did not comment about it. Then we were headed to my place to drop me off.

"Oh dear, What's all this." I commented as I saw all the other vehicles when we drove up to my place. "I hope it isn't a going away party. I don't think I can handle that today!" I commented as I opened the door to the truck and got out.

As we walked toward the door Santa prepared me by saying, "I think it is the bridge builders' conventions!" I stopped and we looked each other in the eyes, as he commented. "I will be here for you if you need me. Are you ready for this?"

I nodded, "let's just do it!"

Buddy was the first to greet me by the back door with a big hug.

"I know what's up!" I commented, "let's get it on!"

I thought to myself it was going to be a long day.

"Outside patio or in the living room?" buddy asked.

"It's a beautiful day!"

I replied as I grabbed a soft drink from the fridge and started heading to the patio. Along the way was a huge bear hug from Gingerboy. He smiled and not a word was said by either of us as I ruffled his Ginger. Some of the people were already out on the patio and I settled into the large lounge chair under the shade of tree.

I was surprised when it started out with a bartender and one of the bouncers from the Buddies Bar. "We don't know much about you, but when you have a few to many lately, you been such an ass that you tend to clear out the bar and drive away all of our paying customers. We are going to go out of business if you do not knock it off" They started in.

"Ginger and Buddy filled us in on what was up and we just wanted to come and see if we can help ya get back on track." They indicated they had seen this happen a lot of times before especially with the veterans from the hospital who were coming back from war.

"Some alphabet soup stuff, what was it called again?" the bouncer asked the bartender and then both chimed in, "PTSD!"

The bartender continued, "We both been there and done that. Until you deal with it, you're restricted to soft drinks only and as far as I am concerned when I am there, they will be on the house."

The counselor from the treatment center was next. He said he could not talk a whole lot about details because of my right to confidentiality. When he shared that sometime intimate details in our lives were the first things to change, he no longer sounded like a perverted rookie.

"Whenever you are ready, you know where to call. Ginger and Buddy are welcome also any time!"

I replied, "Thanks doc, especially for the part on Ginger and Buddy. After what I have done to them, they may need and deserve some attention too!"

Next, a couple of biker buddies gave it their best shot.

"We knew something was up when you talked about abandoning your ole sweet heart (referring to my old Harley that I had for year) and talking about your need for bigger, better and more power. You never were a power freak before. You went from the back of the pack to having to always lead. It was no longer about enjoying the gear and the ride. It was all about how much power you thought you needed or how you had to outdo all of us!"

Another chimed in, "Ya, it was like you no longer liked yourself or anyone else."

Yet another chimed in, "Focus man, LIVE TO RIDE, RIDE TO LIVE!" The tears started to roll as they were hitting a soft spot in my heart.

"Hey, I haven't seen that in a while! Welcome back man! Commented the straight guy who has 3 kids.

I thought I new what was coming next as Buddy's lady friend approached. I started in by saying, "I am so sorry about what I said and what I called you!"

She replied, "Don't worry about it, I am used to ignoring drunk talk! I replied, "Oooh that hurts!" and nodded "It must be truth!"

But she threw a curve ball as she turned it in a different direction. "You have always been a person with enough love to go around for everyone. Your heart was open to all. I knew something was terribly wrong when you were jealous of me."

"I thought I was the one who was supposed to be jealous of you. I was jealous about what you and Buddy had and what the two of you had with Ginger. You guys are super dads with a really really awesome kid. I wanted to learn everything I could from you guys so I could be a super mom for my kids."

She continued on, "Gingerboy saw right thru me. He played me that song that nailed my story. What was it again?"

she asked our boy who replied. "Chain Smokers!"

She continued, "Right! Someone just like this." I wanted super heroes like you guy are. Someone just to love. Someone to kiss. Just someone to miss!" tears filled her eyes

"You don't need to be jealous of me. There is no way in hell that I could take Buddy away from you. After I got to know all of you, I just wanted a piece of all of you in my life. Even when you guys were trying to work thru all of this, I thought you were still my super heroes. Never give up on each other. Now that you are planning to leave, I will get my someone to miss"

When she was wrapping up, she gave each of us a kiss and ruffled up some Ginger hair. "Don't ever loose that love that ya got!"

I began to cry as Gingerboy came up and gave me a hug. "I love you dad!" he started out. "I loved you the first time you ruffled some Ginger. "he stated as he ran his fingers thru his own hair. "I knew then I had something to hook ya with and real you in. You really did get into me. You made me the center of your universe. No matter what obstacle I put in the way you still loved me, cared for me and made sure my needs were met even if that meant yours were not being met. You and buddy both loved me unconditionally like no other person has loved me."

"Then something terrible happened to you. Recently you did things that hurt and I thought I hated you. I began to hate you just like I hated my first parents. Then I started to hate myself again. Hate was starting to win again and I was starting to be a looser again." He sobbed.

When he regained his composure he continued, "As I look back now, I see the pattern. First with my parents, then with my foster home and the group home. Even with my life long friend."

"I first thought you were going to be different. Then this came along and everything seemed to change. It started being just like every time before. I no longer was the center of your universe. I even had to give you rides and take care of you when you were drunk. You said mean things that hurt. You even did things that were meant to hurt. I was really scared and did not know where to turn."

"I sent a text to Santa." Gingerboy continued, "We met and talked. He helped me figure out what has happened in my life. He explained it was like a little snow ball that is rolled down a hill. How one evil deed leads to another. How the snow ball grows and becomes a giant snowball and if you let it go long enough it turns into an avalanche no one can stop it until it crashes at the bottom and leaves a horrible mess. Hatred brings us all down and makes us all a big terrible mess."

Gingerboy continued on, "I remember how you helped me so much by telling me about your journey to finding love. You demonstrated to me how it worked by unconditionally loving me to the best of your ability. Loving me until I could love myself again and then letting go so, I could move on in life and love others."

His speech started to break up and he started to sob, "I don't want us to be losers again! I want us to love again and be winners again!"

He then seemed to steal himself and with determination continued, "I still love you dad and I know you still love me too. We have to let the warmth that comes from our love melt those God damn snowballs before they get out of hand and make us a mess again."

With tears running down my face, I nodded and replied, "INDEED!"

Gingerboy had me in tears throughout much of what he was saying. The famous line ran thru my head, "and a child shall lead them." It felt like he was giving back to me the medicine that I had been giving to him. The love that can cure us all.

So far it had been a very long day. But it was like the cake was just finished and taken out of the oven. There was a little cool down time before the frosting could be added. I asked for and was granted a time out. I took the opportunity to go to the bathroom and stop by the fridge on my way back. Others also scramble to do the same thing I was doing.

Getting ready. It was about time to put some icing on that cake.

Buddy started out with a tender kiss on the cheek and a big strong embrace. I thought to myself here we go. He is starting out with his usual approach. Like his favorite song 'PROUD MARY' he would start out nice and easy and finish it up nice and rough.

He began by asking, "You remember the time when Gingerboy's team won the championship." I thought I knew where he was going with this. I thought about the intervention we had with Gingerboy's friend. It was very much an exhausting and yet exhilarating day like today.

He continued, "Remember the part toward the end of the day when the coach came out and told us what the boy were doing in the locker room?"

He knew he needed to say no more about that as he saw the light come on in my head. I also notice Gingerboy blush and begin to fidget a little bit more over in his chair. He settled and relax with a big sigh of relief as Buddy continued on and did not expose him any further.

Remember shortly after we met how we were in the shower room by the Scuba class pool.

"Do we really gotta go there?" I asked and he nodded, "Oh ya!"

I announced to everybody in the room, "hang on folks this is going to get ruff faster than I thought it would!"

"Do you remember what I had to say to you" he asked

"Oh ya!" I hesitated to say anything more and he responded, "JUST DO IT! Go ahead and tell them!"

Everyone in the room except for buddy burst into laughter when I report to them, "He told me that for a gay guy, I had a pretty big one!"

Ginger boy leaned forward in his chair and then chimed in, "I can picture this!" to which I replied to him, "You don't want to go there! But hang on tight because this rides about to get more interesting!"

Buddy then said "You tell them the rest of the story. You are the better story teller in this family!"

I took a deep breath and continued, "After he complimented me on my big size, I started to show off what I thought was my big dick. He let me show it off for a couple of minutes. I was really getting into this. Then he said 'no! You big dummy. I was talking about your ass!' I thought about it for a second or two while I tried to restore my fragile broken ego and then started to flaunt and show off my big ass until he snapped it with a towel."

Everybody was roaring with laughter.

"But he didn't stop there." I continued to tell the story, "He proceeded to brag on how much bigger his dick was and began dancing just like I had. To which I came back with 'your ass is bigger too.' And he started shaking his butt. I joined in commenting, 'at least I got better dance."

I paused for all the laughter to stop. "that's when I knew I had a really good friend and I loved him! Since then I never stopped loving him"

Buddy chimed in, "now it is my turn!" He took a deep breath as he continued. "Between you and me around here lately, I cannot tell who has been the biggest ass or the biggest dick!" he paused. "I think Gingerboy got it right! Do you want to get back to loving each other?"

Tears came streaming down my face and I replied, "INDEED!"

We embraced again and the room applauded. Soon Gingerboy, crying, put his arms around both of us.

Later that night in the bedroom, we turn our lives around. We were both little boys again. We started to play with each other's dicks and assholes. **We stopped being assholes and dicks.**

IN THE CLOSET

The night before we were going to leave on the move north, we let our son have some friends over and let them use the downstairs of the house. We had already packed up all the stuff we planned on moving with us. Sufficient furnishing remained for our use and would remain with the property when we left.

We made it clear to all of the guests and their parents that they had to live by the house rules.

1. Only consenting adults are allowed to engage in sexual acts with other consenting adults and these acts must take place where they cannot be observed by any minors.
2. Only adults can use tobacco products on the property but outside of any structure or in the designated smoking area (the garage away from combustible products)
3. No illegal drugs or any other illegal activities
4. Limited amounts of alcoholic beverages can only be consumed by adults.
5. Other rules may be set by the adults in the house to assure the safety and welfare of the occupants and guests.
6. Fire is permitted only in the designated location under adult supervision.

Violation of the rules would bring consequences up to and including eviction (sent home)

We were surprised that 24 guests showed up of which 15 stayed overnight. We had to pick up extra Pizza for that many. They had all been instructed to bring their own sleeping bag if they were staying overnight.

Buddy and I would randomly spot check throughout the night to assure everyone was appropriate and safe. We did not encounter any problems during the night. At least we thought that. The next morning the remainder of the parent arrive at the designated times to pick up their kid. Some of the parents work night shifts and we allow those kids to remain until the parents were off work.

There were only three kids remaining when I began missing Gingerboy. Two of the boys were going to be picked up soon. The other was Quarterback who was going along with use for the summer.

Gingerboy did not respond when we called for him. The other boys got rather quiet rather quickly. Buddy and I were about to split the boys up into two groups and go looking for Gingerboy.

Quarterback said, "Ahh, SIR we gotta tell you something."

He continued, "He did not respond when you called because he is tied up right now."

What is he doing that is so important that he cannot come for breakfast? I asked.

Quarterback responded, "You did not understand me. When I said he was tied up I meant literally."

I had a sinking feeling somewhat yelled "What's going on!"

Long story short, one thing led to another. He said sometimes he wished he could go back into the closet. They were having a good time.

He went on and on until I shouted out "Where the heck is he!"

"He is back in the closet!" they chimed in. I knew they were taking me serious at this point because they forgot to say "Jinx!"

"Show us where he is!" I said in a very stern voice.

We went from the family room into Gingerboy's bedroom. I did not see him there.

"Where is he," I asked again. "He is back in the closet" and they pointed to the door. Sure enough, he was back in the closet all tied up in football gear, blindfolded and gaged.

I paused for a moment. Because of his size they could have not done this without him letting them. I had to ask anyway to make certain. I asked the other boys first and they said he consented to this.

I then turned to him. Can you answer yes or no questions Gingerboy?"

"uh ha" he mumbled from under the mask.

"Did they do this without your permission?" I asked.

"unt ah" he replied. To which I responded

"Good thing! They did not violate false imprisonment rules."

The two of you go up with Buddy and finish you breakfast and get ready for you parents to pick you up. Quarterback asked, "Should I go with them?"

I replied, "No, I need you here!"

As for you Gingerboy, you get to stay where you are for a while as a natural consequence for this. Do you understand that?" I asked.

"Uh ha" he replied. Are you in agreement with that consequence? "uh ha".

I replied "GOOD!"

"Listen up both of ya! First and foremost, if you ever do something like this you must look out for the safety of the person. You must never leave them unattended. If something happens to them when you do this you are liable and possibly guilty of murder if the die. Go ahead and take that mouth piece off!" I paused as the quarterback removed it.

"The mouthpiece is rather dangerous item. If the person started to get sick, they would choke on their own vomit and be dead in minutes. Never use a mouth piece unless you can get it off in seconds."

As Quarterback removed the mask I asked, "Are ya alright son!"

he replied "uh ha"

"WRONG ANSWER BOY!" I shouted at him.

"When you get yourself into a spot like this one, the only correct answer is always "SIR YES SIR!"

I paused for a moment, "Now let's try that one again. Are you alright BOY?"

"SIR YES SIR!" he replied.

"Much better" I commented as I ruffle some Ginger.

"SIR, THANK YOU SIR!" he responded to the ruffle.

"Oh, you really are good at this! Your answer surprised even me. Have you had more experience at this?"

"SIR, YES SIR!" he replied.

"I kind of expected that. Is this a real consequence or are you getting too much pleasure out of all this?"

"UM, Sir yes sir, kinda both sir!" he replied.

I then asked, "Would you like to talk more about this with your dads on the trip north?

"SIR, YES SIR!

I got in his face to where he could feel me breathing and stated.

"OK, Time out or games over. Is that your true feeling son?" I asked.

"Ya dad. I would like to share more with ya and learn more from ya! I kinda tried from time to time but I am still kind of embarrassed to be talking about it with my parents."

I replied, "That is kind of a good sign for a kid your age and a difficult topic like this, but please put that embarrassment aside and come to me or Buddy any time you got a question or any time you want to share something.

Remember I would rather here it from you than hear it about you!"

"Now one other important thing." I paused and took the blinders off. He looked at me "What dad?"

"What house rule did you break? Either one of you know?" They both had a puzzled look.

"The living in a fish bowl talk we had last week when we talked about this party."

To which Gingerboy replied "oh ya, that one!"

Quarterback was curious, "Tell me, I must have missed that one!"

to which I replied "I think you probably did. Take it Gingerboy!" I indicated.

"it's kind of a long story and I gotta piss. Can ya get me out of here and I can tell him later?" he asked.

I looked at him and said "Did you put a diaper on before they tied you up?"

"Uh, no sir!" He sheepishly replied.

"Quarterback, go get some towels and run to garage to get a tarp to put under him! And hustle!" He jumped and went to get what I requested.

"You guys are still rookies! You didn't plan ahead for this part! I hope we don't get the carpet wet and end up having to clean it up!"

"You guys did not use slip knots either!"

I commented while working feverously to loosen the ropes.

"so, this is going to take quit a while!" I commented as I continued working on the knots.

"Are you about to have your first watersports event?"

"No dad!" he replied.

"What I mean dad is no not the first time, but yes dad I am about to piss my pants. He calmly said.

It wasn't long before the carpet needed some deep cleaning. He was about to finish up when Quarterback and Buddy came in with the tarp.

"To late! Go get the carpet cleaner!"

NORTHBOUND

§

With two vehicles, one trailer and four drivers this was one of the easier trips north. Only adults could drive the trailers. We all got our passports on time to cross the borders. We showed all the passports, showed the permission slips and any other paperwork they requested and the Canadians were nice enough to let us in after we properly answered all of their questions.

We only drove during daylight hours which were getting a lot longer the further we drove north. We had reservations at lodges along the way. We set up a driver rotation plan so no one had to drive more than 4 hours at a time. We also rotated passengers so we would not get sick of each other's company. We tried to stay in line of sight of each other as much as possible. We also were on the phone frequently talking with each other, especially the two boys. The Pick-up with the trailer took up the rear and the other pick-up lead the way. We got to the point where we could trust the two boys in their own vehicle. After all, they had driven on their own before we left. We just wanted to check if they could do the longer distances.

As we drove along the spine of the Canadian Rockies, the boys were impressed with the awesome beauty. This route was a little slower but we wanted them to be able to see all of this. We had a step by step book for them to follow as to where we would be going and they with GPS did a very good job of navigating. It was a new skill they picked up in a hurry.

I finally got a chance to be alone with Gingerboy when I was driving. I wanted to have a good conversation with him without distracting his driving. We started out with a talk about the upcoming football and school year. When that subject ran out, I popped the big question.

"Show me your hands!" I requested.

"Why?" he asked as he held them up.

"Oh, I just wanted to see how your sex life has been lately!"

He punched me, "DAD!"

I then continued, "I know, I'm not the best at this kind of thing!"

He replied, "I actually liked your style. That was a very start!"

"Why thank you for the compliment. But let us keep focused on the issue at hand!" I replied

"Another good one! Was the hand pun intended or did it just happen again by accident?" he asked. "Oh, that one was actually an accident. So, tell me what's been up?" I continue.

"Man, you are driving me nuts. You really are on a roll here! I had a puzzled look and he continued, "You said, what's been **UP!**

I replied, "Oh I get it!"

"You are actually pretty close to summing it up." He continued.

"for me it pretty much has been a hands-on thing. No exchange of body fluids so I know I am safe so far. Majority of the time it is me and these two guys." As he held up his hands again. "I have tried some mutual hand play. I have had a couple guy handle my butt. I even spent some time with an older lady!

I chimed in "double WHOA, on that one! How old? And you a lady's man?"

He replied, "Only two years older. And ya dad I am still keeping my options open because I am not completely certain yet. You also know everything that went on with Quarterback. We have just been close friends again since the championship thing. We actually like it better that way. We both have 'oral sex'—that means we just talk about it a lot!"

"Tell me what happened with the closet thing?" I asked.

"Well there is whole lot that is going on that I really don't understand yet and not sure if I ever will. I kinda like the high I always get off the gear thing. I feel bigger than I am when I gear up. In a way, others see me that way as well. Like in school if you are a jock, you get put up on a pedestal. Your kinda made out to be a mini super hero. But the way I feel about myself is by far the most important aspect.

I really haven't figured out the tied-up part yet. I really like it but I don't really get it yet. I think sometimes I just like someone else to take control and I have no choice but to just go along. One time in the locker room a bunch of guys grabbed me and gagged me so I could not yell out.

Some of them took turns pissing on my cup. It was all a big control thing for them. It kind of shocked even me that I really liked it. Also, after it happened, it seemed to help me deal with all the other torment, teasing, bullying that was going on in my life. I just resolved myself that they could even piss on me and I still was not going to change who I was.

"Now your turn!" Gingerboy snapped at me. "If I gotta share about me it is only fair that you have to also! Besides, I think you got a whole lot of experiences that you can help me out on. I got that feeling by the way you dealt with me in the closet." He continued, "How' things in you and buddy's bedroom?"

I thought a minute before I replied. "First and foremost, you remember me telling you that I was never going to abuse you! I totally believe that a child has the right to never see their parents doing it. To me that is a lifelong irrevocable right!"

He replied, "Ya I gotcha on that and I really appreciated that, but please tell me more in a way that can help me out a bit here!"

Well, I sighed. "Back to your first question. Things with me and buddy are back to where they should always be!"

He replied, "Great!! You guys really had me very worried recently."

I replied, "That is probably a great place to start with lesson one. Even I am still a rookie when it comes to that part. "it was like other things in life can come along and get in the way of what goes on in the bedroom. It can even get to the point where it can impact on your performance if ya get what I mean."

To which he replied, "Ya I getcha on that!"

"Sometimes, especially with casual sex, it can all just be about performance. But in a long-term lasting relationship it has to be about the love you share with the other person. Sometimes that becomes the toughest part. It's not just up to you! If it is just up to you head to the bathroom and let your mind and these guys handle it." I said as I waved my hands and quickly put them back on the steering wheel.

"See, even driving distractions happen to me." "I did not want to have this kind of talk with you while you were behind the wheel!"

"Oh God you are so right! He promptly replied. "That would have been a sure disaster!"

"Where were we?" I asked and thought for a moment.

"relationships and distractions!" he prompted.

"Right!" I replied.

"See how easy that distraction changed our focus!" He nodded and I continued on. "Well distractions in life and in the bedroom can come along just like that as well!"

I paused briefly. "But I think I was also talking about partnership and relationships. It ain't going to work unless you are both there very good at pretending. I have never gotten that pretending part perfected. The only place I seem to be great at it is with the gear thing. Like you, that is where I am pretending to be much more than I think I am!"

"Okay, now a quiz for ya! I wanna see if you are getting this lesson right?"

I went on. "What is the biggest sex organ on the human body?" I asked.

"That is a tough one." He replied, "There are so many different things that can turn you on. Head of your penis. My balls or nipples. Heck, even my ass hole can to it for me! He replied.

"Close but no cigar yet! You kinda are on the right track though. What are they all wired to?" I hinted

"I get it the brain!" he replied.

"BINGO!" I yelled. "Without your head up here," I ruffled my hand in his hair, "the head down there ain't up for anything!"

"But it can also be a very tricky thing!" I continued on. "Have you ever had a time when someone was doing something to you and it surprised you how much it turned you on even if you really hated it?"

He replied "been there! Done that!"

I continued. "things can happen to our body that really turn us on! We are wired that way. You or someone rubs your dick, all kinds of chemicals are getting released all over your body."

"I learned that again because of that recent events" I continued. As a tear ran down my face.

Gingerboy picked up on it right away and replied "Oh dad you don't have to pick that scar!"

He knew what I was talking about and I replied. "It's ok now and if your ok with it I may be ready to talk about it but only if you are?"

He replied "I been curious about it! I wanted to find out what that must be like!" But if this shit gets to tough for either of us, we will have to call for a time out!"

"Ginger!" I paused. "I pray to God that you will never have to find out for yourself!" Tears were now streaming down my face.

"just in case it ever does happen to you, I want to share about what happened to me. When shit happens the only good thing, we can do with it is to turn it into fertilizer. The only way I can do that is by sharing this in hopes that others can learn from it too!"

I took a long pause and drove a couple miles as we both sat quietly. I said, "Ready!"

We both nodded and commented. "Let's just do it!" "JINX!" He yelled.

"Ah, you win that one!" I replied.

"Here we go! The thing that really scared me the most about it was that I had a huge hard on after it was all over. That is what really scared me the most. All of the Adeline and the power rush was so addictive. At the same time, I was thinking to myself that this was so much not me! I paused. I noted that Gingers eyes were just glue onto me. I wasn't sure what was in his head and I had to check.

"Ginger, where are you at with this so far? I don't want to hurt you with any of my shit." I asked.

"Oh, I am ok. I want to hear so much from you.

Even I could see how that power thing was eating you alive. You are so right about it not being you!" He replied.

"It was really killing me inside that I could kill someone. What made it even worse for me was that he was just a kid."

"Some days I thought maybe it was me that should have died. The counselor told me that was part of the PTSD called survivor guilt. It usually happens like when you are in a plane accident where all of you family dies and you are the only one left. Counselor said it was happening between me and that kid."

"The counselor also said that having some Ginger around in my life made it even rougher. The kid I killed was also a Ginger but a slightly lighter shade than you. He also was a couple years older than you. Even with that I could picture what it could be like if that were you. He must have had parents who probably loved him. I thought how much it would tear me up if I ever lost you!"

By now the tears were streaming down both of our faces. "I gotta pull over for a bit! Call the other car quick!" Soon we pulled into a scenic turn out that had an awesome view of the mountains. It reminded me of Santa and Steamboat rock where we had first met. Where he taught me that he had to pull over and not let the tears in his eyes blind him to the road ahead. Buddy was aware of that and we shared more about it with the two boys.

After I composed myself, we were heading down the road again. Before we left Ginger was digging a bag out of the back. Santa had given Gingerboy that bag about the time we were leaving. He also instructed him to use it for the appropriate season to remind us of our special love.

"Whatcha got there?" I asked Gingerboy as we started down the highway

He replied, "The thing Santa gave us when we were leaving. He told me to open it when the time was right and you could tell me the rest of the story about it!"

I replied, "Just do it!" Soon he pulled out three needlepoint Christmas stockings with each of our names on them.

"Oh shit! You have to be kidding me!" I comment as tears again ran down my cheeks, "Oh he really didn't need to do that for us!"

To which Gingerboy replied, "When he gave it to me, he said I could show it to my dad when we had some time to talk and he would tell me the rest of the story!"

THE REST OF SANTA'S STORY

"What is the rest of the story, Dad?" Gingerboy asked.

"About Christmas time after I went out to the ranch with him and his dogs, he invited me over to his place. He said he had something for me. When I got in the house, he brought me over to the computer and showed me a picture. He said he remembered that special first Christmas after his wife passed away. He said he knew it could be tough if he did not prepare for it properly and keep moving on down his life's road.

"For some reason God took her first and left me behind". Santa said

He went on to say God probably did that because Santa's work wasn't over yet. He pulled up a picture that showed me a bunch of stocking that he gotten from the dollar store. He filled those stockings and brought them out to the school where you had been and gave one to each of the kids. He said that was his way of moving on in life and keeping his life meaningful. He told me my life would be so much more because of the love I share with others. I asked him for a copy of the picture so I could I share it with you. His printer wasn't working so he wasn't able to get a copy. We both must have forgotten about it.

"OMG! Gingerboy shouted. "Santa never forgets me!" He said as tears started to stream down his face. He proceeded to show me a piece of paper that he just pulled out of the stocking with 'Gingerboy' written on it.

"He did remember!" I said as I recognized the picture.

"He also wrote and note on it. Read it to me!"

Gingerboy read the note, "May your stocking always be filled with love" and it was signed SANTA.

As we continued down the highway, I shared with Gingerboy the rest of the story about the stockings and about my time with Santa.

"Santa told me that his wife started all of this." I continued. "She made a needle point Christmas stocking for their first-born son. By the time their second child was born she had arthritis and was not able to finish the stocking she started. She showed Santa how to finish it."

"After that they adopted 4 boys just like we adopted you. But it did not end there. He went on to make each of his grandkids a stocking. He had some of them hanging in his home but the rest had been given to the kids now that they had a place of their own where they were being loved.

"We must be part of his family now! He told me he had only made them for his family."

Gingerboy now shared something else I was not aware of. Santa had told me all about his 40 years with his wife. He did not tell me that the date and time of their wedding was March 18 at 1pm. That date and time on their 40th anniversary was when Buddy stepped in to save my life. That was the last time they had together. That had to be another God thing I thought to myself.

Ginger boy then shared how Santa made him feel so special. "Frequently Santa would come out on his motorcycle. Some times for other business and sometimes just to see me. I told him I wanted to be a biker cop when I grew up. He said that was awesome. He said I have to focus on my school now and do everything I could to make that dream a reality. He said I would have to make all the right choices to keep on the right highway to achieve that goal."

Now it was Gingerboy's turn to have the tears running down his face. "One time I asked him if I could wear his leather vest. He took it off right away and put it on me as well as his gloves and helmet. When he needed to leave, I asked if I could keep the vest. It was very cold out and he needed it to get home so I did not get the vest. But to my surprise, within an hour he was back and handed me a 'hand me down' vest that fit me."

"For some reason that does not surprise me." I replied. "I gotta tell ya about getting pull out of the mud!" But before I do that look up a song on the net for me and play it. Ed Sheeran's song 'SAVE MYSELF"

GOT TO SAVE MYSELF

———————§———————

Gingerboy replied, "ED SHEERAN-SAVE MYSELF. Here it is!" He commented as he fiddled with the pick-ups entertainment system.

I commented, "I first listened to this song when Santa helped me get my poop in a group. It was playing on his stereo as we drove back from the ranch. When I heard the words, I thought he had picked the song for me to hear. He said it just came up at random. As we listened to it, Santa said 'it has to be a God thing!' and My reply to him was that it was talking to me! You gotta here it!"

It started to play that now ole so familiar song—

After the music stopped, Gingerboy commented, "That is profound!" "INDEED!" I replied.

It spoke to me like no other song have ever done before. As I listen to it, I think it may be the voice of God speaking to me.

'GAVE AWAY THE OXYGEN' started me thinking about the diving and what happened with the boy.

"WE DON'T EVEN SPEEK" after I killed the kid buddy and I stopped talking to each other about important things

"Life can get you down so I just numb the way it feels
I drown it with a drink and out of date prescription pills"

"I could see that part!" Gingerboy comment.

"Ya, that is the part that really nailed me!" I replied.

"I'll go back to where I'm rescuing a stranger
Just because they needed saving"

"Got me to thinking about Santa and what he was doing for me!" I commented and Gingerboy chimed in, "Ya he did the same for me!"

Here again between the Devil and the danger

"I was thinking about suicide. I was hanging between death and life. Death was the devil and life was the danger of having to live with all that pain." I began to sob again.

"Ginger, the only reason I was hanging onto life was because I love you so much. But because I could no longer find a way to love myself, I was starting to fuck that up too!" I confessed "I have played that song over and over since that day I first heard it. That was the same day you guys did the intervention on me! You guys said it loud and clear that you all still loved me and the song told me what I had to do. I HAD TO LOVE MYSELF. That song, really was a God thing meant for me!" I concluded.

INTERMISSION

$\rule{2in}{0.4pt}\,\S\,\rule{2in}{0.4pt}$

"Hi everyone! I said as I greeted all the people who are still reading this story. "I am the story teller in this book. I first got picked because I was the one in the blue coveralls in the photo that inspired this book. The author saw that picture on line and read the original comments that had been posted. Buddy is the guy you see in the dry suit in that picture. He narrated the first chapter. By the end of that chapter he was unconscious and I had to take over telling the story until he regained consciousness. After being in the hospital he seemed to be a lot quieter kind of person. He let me take over the narration of the rest of the story and he would interject his insights from time to time. Why did the author pick the two of us? Possibly because we are the same age as he was when he was a Scuba diver. To this day he still wishes he could put on gear like us and go deeper. I think he pick us because he wants the readers to all get a little deeper into the lives of each other. To find out who people really are. Perhaps to tear some barriers down and build some bridges up. I think he deliberately made us gay in a twisted way to try to get us to set prejudice aside and let love prevail. You the reader will determine if that worked.

Buddy and I are both fictional characters. Without the author's imagination we would not exist. Oh, bits and pieces of us come from a lot of different characters who the author has met during his life. But mostly we just are imaginary characters that only live in the authors head. The same is true of all of the other characters in this story. We are all taken from bits and pieces of the authors life or just made up based on a picture he saw on the internet. If you the reader sees a piece of you in this story, the author must think a lot of you. But read on because that character is not all you. We all have pieces from many people in his life or in his head.

While some of the locations are as obvious as what you are reading in front of your face others may not be so clear. Here again the author took bits and pieces of a variety of places. So, if you thought you were up in the Arctic and then suddenly saw a palm tree---Well get over it!! After all this is fictional and that is why you are reading it. If he wrote a book about reality it would not be believable given the current state of conditions, we live in. Hopefully, as you read this story you found it to be believable because it is about the human condition that we all find ourselves in from time to time.

Oh, a big shout out to ED. All the characters of this story loved his songs. As you can see, Gingerboy, Quarterback, and Santa messed with PERFECT and perfected it to fit for Buddy and my anniversary song. If anything, ED we hope even more people buy your albums because of this story. The Author also say thanks for singing such awesome songs. When he first lost his wife of 40 years those songs really spoke to his heart. He repeatedly listened to them even though they brought tears to his eyes just like they are doing this very minute as they run thru his crazy head.

To other singers and song writers whose works show up in this 'fairy tale'. They also had an impact on the author's life. It is hoped they still have impact on the lives of others. The Author hopes they were appropriately placed for the best impact. But we had trouble with AMERICAN PIE. We all like the song but just did not find a place where it would fit into this story.

Today the author has gathered all of the characters here to give them a chance to provide input. The author isn't quite finished with the story. He wanted some of our input as to where our lives take us from this point. After all, he feels it would not be fair to his readers to just let them dangle and make up their own conclusion. HMMM—Maybe that is a good Idea!

Gingerboy, what do you think? You still have much of your life ahead of you. The author has toyed with the idea of making you a pro football player. Give you successes beyond your wildest dreams. After all you were a star player in high school and went on to college with a scholarship. You could grow up to become the first openly gay center in the NFL. Man, what a story that would be!

Or you could be just like every kid regardless of how old they were, who he strived to make life just a little better each day by loving them regardless of what was going on in their lives. Perhaps his biggest prayer will come true and you will simply be a better father than the one that God gave to you!

Gingerboy replied, "Ya, but I have my doubt that I could ever be best dad when I had two best dads. I see a lot of option open to me in this story. I am so young that I have not totally made up my mind on a lot of things even my sexual preference. After all the author did hint that I could even turn out to be a lady's man. He also pointed out that a kid my age should not be boxed in by labels such as gay, bi, or straight. After all human beings are sexual creatures and our personal choices and preference could evolve over time. Perhaps it is all a genetic thing. I hope the biggest message that people get out of my character is that we all need to be loved. Hatred and bigotry after all are the two things that will fill hell the fastest. Just look how bad things got for use in this story when things got in the way of us loving others. Real people in real places are actually doing bad shit to each other and it is tearing their lives apart. The hate is also tearing our country apart as well. Only by embracing love can our lives get better.

Gingerboy continued on— The other thing I like about the story is how he used you, ya you story teller. Look how he wanted to end the practice of thinking that gay Christian was an oxymoron. He also wanted the gay people to stop beating up on God. Don't blame God because some asshole at some time in your life banged the Bible over your head in an effort to beat Christianity into you. A loving God would never do that to you. Those people's Gods are not the real God! The real God loves all of us and wants us all to find that right highway for us to travel down.

"How about you Buddy?" Gingerboy commented. "I think I am done. I may add more later if I think of anything else. But you go ahead and take a turn now!"

"Well, yawl know I am a bit softer spoken than the story teller!" Buddy started in, "I am even softer spoken than I was as a kid! My life started out thinking I had all the answers. Did you ever meet anyone like that? They think they got it all figure out and then boom!! Along comes the love of their life and their lives take a whole new direction. I like how I was able to rethink everything I thought was right.

The majority of honest guys will admit to themselves that they did have that one special person in their life that they could have "gone gay for". Some of us have to admit there was more than one. That is not about being gay, it's about being able to unconditionally love a special person.

I like it how the author made my character strong enough to be willing to risk my own life to save a person that I love even if he was actually still a stranger to me at the time, when I first met him. Even when I was struggling to comes to grips with who I was and who he was. I hope the author showed how my early assumption and prejudices can be set aside when I got to really know the story teller as a real person.

"Well, who should I pass it off to?" Buddy asked. "Hey Quarterback, can you catch this one!"

"Ya I got it! I never fumbled a handoff from Gingerboy—RIGHT! I can handle this one two. Oh, by the way. I want to thank the author, story teller, buddy and Ginger for letting me ride along when they made that big move back north. That is such a beautiful place to see and it was a great opportunity for me. I do still have one request of the author. I wonder if you could let us take a trip up to the Arctic Ocean to go skinny dipping. I think the author had that one on his bucket list at one time. I sure would enjoy doing something like that before my part in the story is over. Oh ya, can you also make me a pro football player too? If Gingerboy and I could be on the same team that would be totally awesome. I know your not completely finished with this yet so I hope you consider some of those options.

Oh ya! Tell my dad thanks for getting in my face at the intervention. Some times dads just have to do stuff like that. Also, Gingerboy, a lot of guys out there have a childhood friend who was really special in their lives. They grew up together from preschool and some how grew apart. Or they could have even been like the author who had a great high school buddy. Like me the author was the lesser character in their high school yearbook while his buddy was a big star. But when his buddy was dying from cancer years after they had last seen each other, he shows up at the door step for one last visit. Thanks to his mom for making that special moment possible by keeping in touch with both of them. My mom was super that way as well. You should include that in this story also!

Mom, you just had a cameo appearance. You always would say "boys will be boys" well I have one for you! Mom's will always be Mom's!! Many times, they are the biggest superheroes and yet they take a back-seat role in the stories of our lives. I think I will pass this off to Buddy's friend the Gym lady!

Good pass Quarterback! You were good at throwing the ball in the story and you did a good job here. You are a great team player for letting us see into your life. Letting us see that a super hero like a Quarterback can be a fragile human like the rest of us. Also, how you can bounce back from a challenge in your life and get back up to be a good team player. Thanks for saying that stuff about moms. I really hope it helps all the readers out there to remember their mom. Like me they may not be a super hero. They just got up everyday working and tried to do their best for their kids.

Speaking of which, let me talk about the kid who storyteller had to kill and any other reader out there who may be on the same pathway he was on. That kid was a good kid who just made some terrible choices. Those choices ended up hurting a whole lot of people. Mom's should never have to bury their kids. The author told me about something similar in his life. The simple wrong choice of swimming in a farm pond brought about a tragedy in his life that he lives with to this day. He watched as his mom and the rest of their family had to bury his brother. You could not believe how packed that church was with family and friends. Kids please make the right choices so your loved ones do not have to deal with that pain. I hope the author was able to show how even a stranger like story teller was hurt by such tragic loss of life.

"Touch down!" Quarterback replies. "See what I mean about moms! Every reader out there should be telling their mom "thanks" about now. Even if that mom has gone to heaven! Hay story teller, you have really been a good team player here do you want to take over again!

"Hold on for a minute!" Gingerboy interjected. Let's not forget Grandma and step-dad. They just had a cameo role so far and this story would be so lacking without them. I think the author tried his best to show how a little boy like Buddy can have really tough life events thrown their way. Especially with the loss of a father. All of us try to do their best but some holes just cannot get filled.

Thanks, team, for giving your input on this. There are a couple other characters who could not make it today but they shared their input with me to say with all of you. First CREW CHIEF wanted to say something. If you have power or authority over others don't be an ass about it like he was. He has a favorite saying now—Time wounds all heals! Since when did humans become "expendable assets"?

Secondly, Thanks to the CEO of the company for trying his best to be a person who cared more about needs of people instead of the greed of the industry. He wanted to ask his peers a good question. He wants to know if you can take all the cash profits you make along with you to heaven or the other place if you are heading that way? Just look how easy it was for him help make the lives of people who worked for him much better. Why does 90% of the wealth of the world need to be controlled by 1% of the people.

Now for my personal input. Thank all of you for being here today. Also, thanks to the author for providing us a chance to give our input before the story was over. Without you none of us would exist. At this point in the story I want to thank you for getting me back on the right track so quickly before irreparable damage was done to the ones I love in this story. I could not have done that without the help of "Santa"! Sir, I trust your judgement to treat us all far and God's grace to bring this story to a happy conclusion.

BUCKET LIST

―――――――――――――§――――――――――――――

How can you possibly say no to a request like that! After I shared a story about an ice dive in the Arctic, the boys started talking about how cool it would be to go skinny dip in the Arctic Ocean.

"Do you actually realize how far it is to go to get up there?" I asked them. "Do you realize how freaken far that is."

Gingerboy used my own words against me, "we are supposed to enjoy the journey as much as the getting there".

I guess they learned something from me as I drummed that into them on the drive home from the lower states.

So, one day, just on a lark, we rented some specially equipped motorcycles from a guy we knew and headed up the Dalton Highway. Buddy called ahead and made reservations for the tour ride from Dead Horse to the Ocean. With the 24-hour sunlight we could drive until we dropped. That gravel road is longer than most of the states in the lower 48.

We ran into a biker couple at the Arctic Circle where we all camped overnight. While sitting by the camp fire that evening, they shared with us that they were about to complete a journey from Key West to the Arctic.

"That sounds like it would be such an adventure! We should try it some day Dads!" Gingerboy commented and went on to share our plans, "We're a goin' skinny dipping up there!"

"That sounds so awesome!" One of the bikers replied and the other replied,

"We ought to join'em!"

We found out they would be on the same tour in Dead Horse as we were. So, our 'skinny dipping motorcycle gang' just got bigger.

We all filled up with gas at Cold foot, the last gas station on the highway before Dead Horse. This is where the special bikes come in handy as they are designed to make that distance on a tank of gas. We about ran into a local pedestrian who was crossing the highway shortly after we left the gas station. It was a cow moose and I had done a good job of instructing the boys that when you see one, there is usually a kid tagging along. They missed hitting both!

We were very saddened to see that some assholes had vandalized the 'last tree'. The last tree along the highway was clearly marked. It was very dead and looked like it was a couple years ago that someone had damaged it.

We set up a camp at Lake Galbraith on the north face of the Brooks Range. That is the very last camp site on any US highway or road as you drive north. We took the camp site by the only picnic table in the camp ground and Buddy fixed supper while the boys set up our sleeping arrangements.

"The Arctic Ocean is still a 4 to 6 hours drive depending on traveling conditions on a gravel road." I commented, "We need to get some sleep here before we go on!"

About 2 AM we watched the sun not set before it started rising in the sky.

At Lake Galbraith, I even got to see a sight I had not seen before. The melting snow created a river that cut into the bank exposing the frozen tundra.

"That is why there are no trees up here!" Gingerboy shared with Quarterback.

Again, he impressed me with how smart he is.

I asked, "Who told you that?"

and he replied, "I just put that all together after I saw the last tree and saw this!"

It all made sense as the layer of dirt above the ice seemed way too thin to support any tree. As we passed by a construction site on the road, we saw them put down several layers of insulation before placing the road on that.

Gingerboy commented "they have to put the insulation down or the heat from the road will melt the tundra. When the tundra melts the roads sink and turn into rivers instead of roads."

Each day the boys would find something fascinating. It was the time of year that was just right to go. Not to cold, 24-hour sunlight, and before all the mosquitos come to eat the tourists.

They should have a sign for this!" Buddy commented as he pointed to a dandelion. He was probably right as we did not see anymore the rest of the way north.

Finally, we arrived in Dead Horse. We had some time to look around before we met our tour group. Deadhorse was an interesting place that I would never want to live. About 6-7 thousand horny straight guys all living in a worker's camp. There also were a few women and my kinky mind thought that the odds were pretty high for them.

We drove our bikes over to the local service station. Gingerboy and Quarterback were impressed that the pumps were inside tiny garages that could be shut up in the dead of winter.

We took pictures of the pipeline that we had been following all the way along the Dalton.

"Is that the ocean?" Quarterback asked when we saw a big lake on the edge of the town.

"No, we got 8 more miles to go!"

$70 apiece got us onto a tour group that took us the final 8 miles from Deadhorse to the shore line. I was glad to see there were no little kids in the tour group we were on. The skinny dipping would have been a challenge if there were any. While Gingerboy and quarterback were still minors, they had seen plenty naked people over the years in the football locker rooms. To make certain this was all ok with them we did ask Quarterbacks parents permission on this. When we asked, they both split up in laughter. I thought his mom was pretty cool as her reply was, "Boys have to be boys!"

With a south wind blowing at 45 mph, the air temperature at 40, and the water temp at 34 the skinny dipping was only a few minutes. To our surprise, we were joined by another much older couple of guys. They shared what their plans were and checked to see if we were ok with that. I smiled and pointed to Buddy.

"You will get along great with that guy!" when they shared that their 'bucket list item' was to dip in the Arctic Ocean with a diaper on. One of them proudly explain,

"I have done this in all of the great lakes and all of the other oceans that touch the USA."

They got to chatting with Buddy and even gave him a sneak peak of their 'Rearz'.

I replied, "Those would be cool to have on long motorcycle rides" because of the skull and cross bone design on them.

After we completed our mission, we sought shelter next to a steep bank that blocked the wind for us. Out of the wind, the sun felt very warm.

"We could pretend to be on a beach in Hawaii!"

Quarterback commented. Gingerboy replied,

"That is too big of a stretch for me!"

"You didn't recognize him?" Buddy asked.

"Recognize who?" I replied because I was clueless as to what or who he was talking about.

"Our tour driver!" Buddy commented. "At first I did not recognize him either because of the beard. The minute he spoke, that voice sounded to familiar! It took me a while to put it all together!"

"OH FUCK!" I shouted as it sunk in who it was.

Buddy warned me keep it cool he is coming over here.

The tour driver came over to us and started the conversation.

"Saw what you were up to over here!"

To which buddy replied, "BUSTED?"

"Oh no, He replied. "You guys are not the first skinny dippers I have seen. But I have to admit those two were the first diaper bABies I have seen here!"

He continued on,

"When I saw your names on the roster, I started to wonder. But it threw me a curve at first because of the other two names on the reservation roster with you (referring to Quarterback and Ginger). If it is okay with you guys and if it isn't too early, I would like to ask you for your forgiveness?" Our old crew chief asked. I looked over at buddy and let him take the lead on this one because he had suffered the most from what this guy had done.

Buddy took a really deep breath and let it out. He lifted up both of his arms as if to give a big bear hug. Tears began to stream down both of their faces. I had never seen that before in the crew chief. After their embrace I offered my hand to shake and said

"I should thank you for sending me with him!" to which he replied,

"No thanks are needed as I was still being an asshole when I did that!" He went on to explain, "Sending you would get both of you off my boat that day."

"Since then I had a real awakening and change of heart." The crew chief continued. "I eventually reached my bottom. All of my prejudice and hate was doing was eating me alive. I lost my job and family because of it. I was wallowing in my self-pity. I was going to end it all. Thank God for sending me an angel to help open my eyes. I got to the point in my recovery where I knew someday, I was going to have to make amends with you guys.

"It was one of my 'Bucket list' things. I had no clue that it would be today." He went on, "heard you guys talking about a bucket list thing!" I then saw a smile on his face for the first time in my life.

After some quiet time alone with Buddy, he invited all of us out to supper. We did not tell Gingerboy and Quarterback, and the other bikers about who he was. We just introduced him as a person we used to work with.

We camped out again at Lake Galbreath. Sitting by the evening campfire Buddy and I shared the rest of the story about what had happened to us and who he was. One of the other bikers shared with us that he had once been just like crew chief. He also went thru a similar change. At the end of our conversation he concluded,

"Perhaps with love we can all change one heart at a time!"

By then buddy had walked off for some quiet alone time. I found him on ice over by the stream and sat quietly next to him. He shared what he and the crew chief had talked about when they had time alone with each other. I just held Buddy and when he was finished, I commented.

"Where do you get all that strength?" He blinked his eyes a couple times and looked up as if he could see into heaven.

As we drove home, we thought what could possibly top this adventure. We somehow kept coming up with more bucket list items to complete throughout our lifetime. How do those crazy thoughts find there way into our heads?

"Wonder what it would be like to skydive wearing just a strap and cup?" Gingerboy asked.

Quarterback's face lite up as he could picture himself in that gear. Then he got the biggest grin on his face and said. "Boys gotta be boys!"

THE CALL OF THE DEEP

Like the call of the wild, the call of the deep never let's go of you. Once you have had a taste of it you want it even more than before. Not being able to dive again was the one thing that really depressed Buddy. He was like Pavlov's dogs, every time my phone would ring, he would start to drool. It had been a while since the accident, when he went in for his checkup.

The doctor said he could not clear him for returning to work as a commercial diver. But the doctor did set up parameters in which he could now go on pleasure dives within his guidelines. We were both so excited when we got that news. I knew how much this meant to him.

The doctor wanted to start at the beginning with pool dives at first and see how well he tolerated that. We all new that would be like smelling the barbeque but not tasting it.

For buddy, "Just getting the gear wet will be awesome!" He commented.

We both knew getting the gear on him and just getting in the pool would be like licking the barbeque sauce off the rib. Sometimes he had been wearing the dry suit for an entire weekend just around the house. He looked forward to rainy days when he would put the dry suit on and go take HARLEY out for a spin.

For the first pool dive we got him into a wet suit.

"The feeling of the water filling my suit is driving me nuts!" he reported as he got into the pool.

"Good! It is doing what it is supposed to do." I replied. "Now you got me thinking about how HOT you will be in bed tonight!"

Which brought some laughter from the friendly spectators who wanted to be here to share this event.

I was surprised that the CEO of my company was one of them there. When he heard about this, he arranged to have private time at the pool.

He was a diver also but his business was such that he did not get into the deep nearly as much as he would like to.

He asked, "How is that daddy mission going for you guys?"

"Oh, he is such an awesome kid. I cannot stop myself from loving him more each and every day." I continued, "Some days he makes me wonder if I am good enough for him and about then he tells me he could not ask for any better dads."

Would you like to meet him?" I asked.

"Oh, hell yes!" The CEO promptly replied.

"Hay kid, get over here!" I yelled out for Gingerboy.

Gingerboy immediately responded with that, oh GOD what now look. To which I prompted him, "Get your butt over here to meet this guy!"

The CEO commented, "He is just like mine who is that age! We should let them meet up!" They shoke hands and exchanged names.

"I got a kid your age. Would ya like to meet him sometime?"

"Indeed!" Gingerboy replied.

I chuckled as I realized how even our language was rubbing off on him.

The CEO continued to proudly share about his son, "He is the quarterback on the local team!"

"NO SHIT!" Gingerboy yelled out loud enough to echo thru the entire pool side area. "I hope I can snap to him!"

"Ah!" the CEO replied, "You're the new kid the coach told us about!"

He shared about the former center on the local team graduated last season. "He really wasn't all that great. He often would get and attitude and deliberately miss key blocks costing the entire team."

Ginger boy felt confident now that he would get plenty of game time this fall. He had been worried about what competition he may be up against for the position. He was pleased to here the position was open and he was already being considered to fill it.

Buddy did as well as we all expected in the pool dive. I shared with the CEO how the gears in my head were turning. "We just met a couple of guys who were traveling from the Keys to the Dead Horse."

I explained. "The boys thought it would be a great adventure. I thought as long as we have to take quarterback back down to the lower 48. It would make sense to go on to the Keys since we were most of the way. I just need to figure out if I can afford the time and cost to do it."

"DONE!" yelled the CEO.

"But here is the deal. I need you down there on an assignment in a couple of days. If buddy and the boys could drive down to meet you there, I would pick up their expenses as well. I think I could give you the time after that to drive back up with them."

"SIR" I reached out my hand to shake his, "You have been way too good to us!"

"Us divers gotta take care of each other!" he replied.

He then stood up and yelled out an order to some other crew members in the building, "Guys, Let's get those boys in some suits! We have to give them a quick course before they go!" He turned to me "If this is all okay with you?" By then my jaw was scrapping the floor and I gave a thumbs up signal.

The boys did not even question what was going on. They were just very excited about getting some gear on and joining buddy in the water. As they figured out, they were being put through a crash-diving course they started to have more questions. But the classroom course and pool side training kept them pretty occupied. They had to learn about all the pressure changes and other safety issues. They also needed to know how to safely use the equipment.

The CEO called ahead to a shop in the Keys that he had frequently been to. He shared with them what was happening and made all the arrangement we would need.

I clued buddy in on what was happening. He called and made the arrangements with Quarterbacks parents. His mom commented, "How are we ever going to live with such a spoiled brat after you guys get done with him?"

The next day I had to keep my end of the bargain. On the plane, my head was racing with all the thoughts about what a great time this was going to be. Once I got there, I had to change focus to the mission I was on.

I about crapped my pants when I found out that my mission was to learn how to be a dive instructor. The CEO wanted me for that position so he could have another trainer. The business was doing so well that he was expanding it. He needed more divers and had to have instructors so he could train them.

The CEO also made arrangements for Buddy to take the instructor course after the time we had with the boys. "This is the perfect opportunity to get him back in the gear!" The CEO commented "You guys are a great team and I want both of you together on my team!"

Just like the Florida Keys commercial said, we were about to let the next chapter of our lives start in the Keys.

THE NEXT CHAPTER

§

While a lot of people who first met us had the impression that I am the one who is dominant in our relationship, in reality Buddy is far stronger and more masculine than I ever was.

In public, buddy was much quieter and we appeared to be peers.

Nowhere was his dominance over me more evident than in our dungeon. That was also true in our bedroom except when we would have a role reversal to let him be the little bABy with me being the father taking care of him. Even in that dependent position he seemed to be in command making me wait on him, get his bottle for him, get his blankie for him, get his teddy bear for him, even change his diaper for him. Kinda like real life where the needs of the child command the actions of its parents.

It should not have come as any surprise to me when the CEO selected him to be in charge in the dive shop. Oh ya—the CEO went into partnership with us to set up a dive shop. He invested about 60 percent and we used some of the settlement money to invest 40 percent. He also gave us the majority of our business by contracting us to train divers for him. I still got calls to go out on other missions while Buddy stayed behind and ran the shop.

While I was initially jealous of the position Buddy had on the shop, I got over it in a hurry. This was really a great opportunity for him and it gave both of us the opportunity to be working with each other again. We could count on having each other's back. It is always great to have a BUDDY whose got your back.

We worried that Gingerboy was not going to recover in time to play football for the second season we were up north. During the summer he twisted up his knee when a car pulled out in front of his motorcycle.

When we got the call, he was in the hospital we about freaked out. We were pleased that he had not gotten hurt any worse.

He seemed to be making many more friends in the new school. Two of his friends seemed to stand out the most. The CEO's son who was a quarterback became a very good buddy. We called him (the CEO quarterback) who came immediately to see Gingerboy. After a brief greeting and time to find out he just had an injured knee, Gingerboy instructed him to, "Call my girlfriend!"

Buddy and I stood in silence initially. We both stared at each other as if the other had not told us this news. Gingerboy must have picked up on what was going on in our heads.

"I did not tell either of you!" He reported.

"I was not sure how you guys were going to take it or how I was going to tell ya!" I was hoping for a better way and a better time than this!"

"Start talking!" Buddy instructed him.

Gingerboy went on to tell how he met this gal at school and she somehow became his best cheerleading, not just on the football field either.

"I am not sure what is going to come of it, but I think I fell in love with her." He commented, "I shared with her who I was and where I have both been in life and she is okay with who I am." He went on to assure us, "I even told her about my two dad's who have been the greatest thing to happen so far in my short life!"

I replied, "OH, are you meaning that or just spreading the butter on a bit thick?"

Before he sidetracked us, I commented, "This is not about us, tell more about you!"

Gingerboy replied, "You know me too well now and don't let me get away when I compliment you!" he did continue "I did mean that compliment!" at about which time his friends came into the room.

After a short embrace of his cheerleader and telling her what happened, he introduced us to her. She came over and gave each of an embrace.

"I have heard so much about both of you. I was really hoping to meet you soon."

To which I replied, "not the best time to meet but let's just make it work!"

She nodded with approval.

"Let's let these love birds alone." Buddy reported after the doctor met with us.

"We left the shop open to run over here. Hope it is still standing when we get back."

I knew full well that was just a line because we had another crew member back at the shop.

I took buddy's hint and went with it after I got assurance his friends would get him home safe. The hospital staff would not let us leave until we signed off on some paperwork. On the way out of the hospital I compliment Buddy, "Thanks for coming up with a good line! For a change I was at a loss for words."

He responded, "That was sure a surprise to me as well!"

STAY IN TOUCH

During Gingerboy's Junior year of high school, the football team made it to the state championship finals. Both teams had been undefeated in their regular seasons. Because both teams were tied at the end of regular season, a flip of the coin decided who would have the home team advantage. We had to fly into watch our team face the Barrow Whalers. The game time was set for noon. It would be under the lights as sun wouldn't rise on the game at this time of the year. While our school was a power house with several past championships the Whalers were more of a Cinderella team. Ginger admitted that as he watched the Whalers in the regular season gain an undefeated record his admiration for them was building.

Ginger even looked up some facts on Wikipedia about Barrow also known as Utqiagvik, which is the northern most city in the USA. It places ninth in the world as farthest north community. Utqiagvik's population of 4,212. The city's native name, Utqiaġvik, refers to a place for gathering wild roots. The name Barrow was derived from barrow point, and was originally a general designation, because non-native Alaskan residents found it easier to pronounce than the Inupiat name. I was very impressed when I heard the part about the community being as old a 500 AD. There are no roads into the community. As we flew in, I was not as impressed with what I could see from the light of a full moon. It was very baron place until we spotted the lights of the community. Anybody who lived in these parts must have a hardy soul. We landed safely at the Will Rogers-Will Post memorial airport.

Our opponents were very gracious meeting us at the airport. They matched up the players with a companion on the other team who played in a same position on the field. We were the guest and our hosts treated us like royalty. I was surprised to find out they had a college whose emphasis was on the teaching of skills needed to survive in the region. The area has a "damp law" that prohibits the sale of alcohol.

"Were fine with that!" I commented.

Gingerboy asked his host, "What do you do here for excitement?"

"Not much!" his host replied. "We did have a Russian Ice Breaker up here one time that came to save some Gray Californians that got lost and stranded up here! That got us on the news for a while!" He continued, "We did not have football up here until our first game back in 2006. It was the first official football game to be played north of the Arctic Circle. After there first win a couple weeks later the team celebrated with a dip in the Arctic."

Ginger replied, "Been there done that!" going on to share about our skinny dipping in the Arctic at Dead Horse a few years back. At that point his host offered a fist bump and Ginger accepted.

"Dude, you are a pretty cool guy! Our host complimented.

I think we had a new buddy.

Ginger commented to Buddy and me, "Do you think Santa would love it here? We are only 1,300 miles away from his home, the North Pole." He had to go on to explain who our Santa was to his host.

I was surprised with all the security around the field. Who would have thought such a force was needed way out here in such a remote area. I come to find out that all of the security was there to keep the real polar bears from entering the arena. We started a conversation with couple of the security guards.

"To us this place looks like a football stadium." The first one commented.

"To the polar bears this is just one giant concession stand!"

"You wouldn't want to become one of their tasty snacks now would ya!" Commented the other. A big chill went down my spine from what he said as well as from the breeze that was starting to blow.

Buddy and I settled in to sit back and watch the game. We jumped to our feet and cheered as our team got the first touchdown. The score went back and forth during the first half. The boys went into the locker room and the game was tied at the half.

When they returned our team had to kick off and the Whalers would receive. They got good field advantage because the kick was shortened by what now was a steady breeze. It didn't take them long to get into the end zone.

Our team seem to hold their own until the Whalers best defense arrived on the field midway thru the third quarter. A frigid blast swept across the field as the winds of the Artic began to blow in our opponent's favor. Our team got to within field goal range. The kick was off, but it just seemed to hang in the air as a stiff wind intensified and the ball fell short on the goal line.

The Whalers returned the ball for another touchdown. I sensed that our team was doomed. Behind by two touch downs on a field where the opponents were accustomed to the conditions and the crowd was in their favor, our fate was sealed. The Whalers made another touchdown and this game was mercifully over.

"It's just down here about the length of a football field!" Gingers host announced as he and Ginger lead the way down and the rest of the team followed for a dip in full football gear. The quick dip in the Arctic Ocean was followed by a quick run to the warmth of nearby locker rooms.

Gingers host commented, "You guys are damn good but no one has beaten us when the OLE MAN comes to play on our team."

Ginger had a puzzled look as his host went on, "OLE MAN WINTER!"

Our hosts were very gracious and invited us to join in a meal of some of the local flavors at the high school cafeteria. Thank goodness they also imported some HOT CHOCOLATE!

While we all moved ahead with our lives, we tried our best to keep in touch with some of the friends we had down in the states. Social media and cell phones made the world smaller and easy to keep in touch. At first, I did not think much of it when we first got a call on Thanksgiving Day. It was Quarterbacks Mom.

She usually didn't call and we had been wondering why Quarterback had not called in a couple of months. His mom sobbed over the phone,

"He had a bad accident on the field. He was tackled in the back and now paralyzed below the waist!".

"Oh shit!" I replied as I sat down and started to sob myself.

She continued on. "He seems really depressed. It is like the script he wanted for his life has been taken away from him. He is lost and doesn't want to go on. He feels his life has ended already."

Gingerboy collapsed to his knees sobbing when we told him. His cheerleader was there and did her best to comfort him.

After we composed ourselves, Buddy announced, "DUDES! We just gotta go see him and try to help him out."

We called quarterbacks mom back to see if we could show up and try to do our best to cheer him up.

"You just gave me something to be thankful for on this Thanksgiving!" she replied.

We made arrangements to spend our Christmas break with them.

It didn't really surprise me when Gingerboy and cheerleader asked if she could go along with us. They wanted to share their first Christmas together. She wanted to provide moral support for Gingerboy. She also wanted to meet in person all of the friends Gingerboy had told her about in the lower states. She also had friended Quarterback on line. She wanted to go along and meet him.

Her parents were very honest with us when we first met to ask if she could go along.

"We thought Gingerboy was a super hero." Her mom stated. "We have not seen cheerleader so happy before. I knew we could not break them up. That would just turn into Romeo and Juliet!"

Her father then chimed in, "We talked about breaking them up, but realized that would not work. We talked with the both of them how we felt. I told Gingerboy he was a super kid in spite of who his parents were."

He paused before he continued on, "Your kid argued with me and tried to convince me that he was a good kid because of your love for him. He told us how you adopted him and how much of a difference you have made in his life."

"After hearing this kid out," he paused to give Gingerboy and quick hug, "I knew I had to give him a chance. Now that I hear what you want to do for Quarterback, perhaps I need to set aside some of past opinions and give you guys a chance as well."

He shared how he was a minister at a local church. He went on to give his daughter permission to go by saying to us, "Don't screw this one up! Be sure you get my daughter back here safe!"

We shared how we had very mixed feelings about going on this trip. We all knew we had to and wanted to go see Quarterback. But what could we possibly say to help make a difference in his life now?

The Reverend indicated, "What you do matters more than what you say!"

We went to the rehab center to visit with him. His mom went in the room and asked him if he wanted to have a couple of quests that she brought along with her. At first, he just sat there very sullen staring out the window. He burst into tears and his face lit up brighter than any star on top of a Christmas tree as we entered the room.

"Oh FUCK!" He started to sob, "I cannot believe you guys came all that way to see me on Christmas Day!"

Sometimes, like this one, just being there for a friend is enough.

SANTA followed us in. "I am sorry kid!" he commented, "I can never out do the gift you just been given."

His voice still breaking from sobs as Quarterback replied, "INDEED!"

We all followed along as Quarterback lead us on a tour of the rehab center.

"This is the spot that seems to depress me the most!" he reported as he stopped at the base of the stairs. There was a bench close by and Santa lead the way to sitting on it.

"Why would a place like this put something like this here?" He asked.

"I have spent a lot of time wondering about it. I thought about my whole life, how I thought I was climbing the stairway to success. But now, here I am stuck at the bottom! I have nowhere to go!" He reported as a tear flowed down the side of his face.

Cheerleader pulled out a Kleenex and wiped his tear away and said, "We just gotta help you find the ramp!"

"That about sums it all up!" Santa said. He then asked a special favor of Gingerboy "Use that thing you got and play me the "**Stairway to Heaven!**"

Tears now ran down all of our faces as the words of this song now had much more meaning to all of us. As the song finished playing, Santa commented. "That was just stuck in my head for some reason. Perhaps someday, God will let me climb that stairway!"

Santa then called upon me to share my story about when I was stuck in the mud. I knew exactly what he was talking about as did most of the people who love me.

"Quarterback, you know much of my story!" I replied, "Why don't you take Gingerboy along and tell cheerleader all about it? While you are at it, try to find that wheelchair ramp to heaven!" I said and continued "I want to spend a little more time with Santa now to get to know him a little better!"

Quarterback replied, "Oh thank you so much sir!" As another tear ran down his face he reported, "There is still time to change the road I am on. Thanks to you guys I can now see the beginning of the ramp that lays ahead of me!"

A month later I got a call from his mom. "I Need to thank you guys for giving me back my son!" After a few tears she went on, "While he knows there may be a long struggle ahead, he also now says he is going to make it because he has a lotta people out there who love him and are going to cheer him on. He said to tell you he found a good place to look to the west." She described a place he goes to each day to watch the sun set and comments that "With all the love he has been shown he knows his road will go on."

SANTA'S ELF

As the two of us sat there alone on that bench, Santa commented.

"I have really missed having you along on the trips out to the ranch. Sometimes I struggle with the loneliness and others I cherish the time to myself. Santa reported.

Whenever I need to be with her (referring to his wife of 40 years), I take a hike up to Steamboat Rock. Sometimes the dogs go along in the truck and sometimes Harley takes me there. Someday you and my other friends will have to take me up there to be with her."

"Not very soon I hope!" was my reply. "Stick around for awhile and let me pick more of that brain of yours."

Santa replied, "I am ready to go any day now. But each day that I think about it, God comes up with another soul for me to rescue. He is not done with me yet."

"I may not be done with you yet either!" I added.

I went on to share what had been happening in our lives.

"Did I tell ya that Buddy and I met the old crew chief?" I continued. "Initially, all of that old rage boiled up inside and I just wanted to strangle him. I had to fight hard to hold it back."

"I was impressed by Buddy." I continued, "He had the balls and the heart to forgive that guy even while he was still dealing with the pain that guy put us thru."

"Sometimes we are called upon to just do it!" Santa replied. "Just forgive. Just let it go and let God take care of it all. God usually does a better job handling it than we do. It is really surprising how much forgiveness is for those forgiving as much as it is for those forgiven."

I shared the joy that was also happening in my life. How cheerleader came into our lives. How it surprised me how much Gingerboy and her love each other.

He replied, "Aren't you the one that says don't box people in with labels?"

"Ya." I acknowledged. "It is still easier to preach than it is to practice."

Santa then asked, "How's things with you and Buddy been?"

"Oh, we still give people a whole lot to gossip about."

I replied and went on to share some of the details. More about the kinky side of our lives without sharing about the details so I would not freak him out. But I felt sure knowing that I could probably share anything and he could handle it.

I continued "But, all of that is just the fringe benefits. You understand how lost I would be without his love in my life."

Santa replied, "Ya I did not know how much that love meant for me until I lost it!"

Santa paused, "How you have something really special to tell and no one is there to listen who would understand what you are meaning. I liked all of the independence to do what I wanted, go where I wanted and do what I wanted whenever I wanted, even by the cloths that I wanted. But then I realized I had to make all those choices and live with the consequences."

Santa continued. "I even tried to find the life that I thought I had lost. Do most of the stuff that I missed doing in my life with her. I have to admit that sometimes it was a lot of fun. But sometimes it left me with the empty feeling that I was trying to fill. In many ways I think I am still on that journey. Right now, I am of the mind that one woman in my life was enough for me. I will get by with a little help from my friends. Santa feels really good when he gives out a lot of hugs. Some day he also needs a hug."

"I need big bear, now!" He concluded as he held out his held out his arms for a big hug.

I lifted him off of the ground with a hug and took a spin. As I let go of him, I applied a couple of pats on his bun like Ginger sometimes does out on the football fields to encourage his friends. "You are going to do just fine ole man!"

FOOTBALL FANTACIES

———————————— § ————————————

Shortly after we first met, Santa had admitted to me that like Buddy he never got to play football.

He said "I grew up on a farm where we had to ride home on the bus every day to be chore boys. I had to tackle smelly ole milk cows instead of smelly jocks. For wrestling we had real swine instead of mud pigs. I got into biking initially because I had a friend who was an only child. His parents tended to spoil him. While I had three brothers, I was my friends only brother. I even ended up naming my first son after him. He was the first guy I crushed on and that probably was because of the motorcycle and gear that he had."

That confession was the first thing that gave me suspicion that Santa may also be a gear freak. Not only did we spend a lot of time out on the ranch, we would also go over to each other's places to have some gear time. Right now, it felt like it was GEAR TIME!

"You want to come over for a while and gear up?" Santa extended the invitation.

"Oh, hell ya!" I eagerly replied.

We tried to clear it with Buddy who was jealous indicating, "I want to go along too!"

Quarterbacks mom overheard our conversation. "Boys have to be boys!" she interjected. "You guys go ahead with Santa and I will give the kids a ride when every they are done visiting."

Three little boys hoped into Santa's sleigh (a red Chevy pickup) and were off to play.

"Gear time!" we all shouted

"Jinx!" Buddy and I shouted.

When we arrived at his place Santa showed us some of the recent additions to his collection. "Got this one that has my high school colors and Cardinal mascot.

It really goes well with this gear. He showed it off with a protective pad that had the company name on it. The company name was the same as Santa's real first name. His Cardinal Jersey had his last name printed above the numbers.

"Santa, you always did look great in red gear!" I complimented as we all laughed.

"HO, HO, HO! You know I had to say that.!" Santa chimed in.

Like three little boys in a candy store we dug in. We tried on various outfits until we settled in on our favorite. There were occasional butt slaps to show our approval of the gear we were putting on. Santa even had some Rearz and other adult underwear that we liked.

Santa definitely looked best in red. Buddy was great in black and white. It was a little more difficult to decide what best fit me. I liked all of them a lot.

Santa would have gotten first prize when he suited up in Red with black leather and hopped on Harley. All being the fans of the same NFL team we loved what he had done to his master suite.

We even tried out some of the hockey and other gear Santa has in his collection.

We all agreed that Quarterback's mom was right when she said, "Boys have to be boys!"

TO MRS. CLAUS

Buddy and I took some special time out and went back to be with Santa on the 18th of March. While it was Buddy and my anniversary of the incident on the ship it was also Santa and Mrs. Claus's wedding anniversary date. Santa brought out a picture book that he had made. Each picture had a short-written description of the picture. As we paged thru the pictures Santa shared more about each picture and about that time and his life together with Mrs. Claus.

Santa shared how he had been worried that Mrs. Claus would leave us on Thanksgiving.

"I was worried she would die on one of the holidays. I did not want that to happen and have the family remember the holiday with sorrow."

He went on to share that he asked God,

"Please let her stay at least until we are past the holidays. While you are at it, if you're really listening and if you really do have a big heart let us have our 40ᵗʰ anniversary together!"

Santa went on to say, "I did not think much about that as we just struggled to get through each and every day."

He continued, "It really sank into me that it was a GOD THING when the last day we had to share with each other was our 40ᵗʰ anniversary on the 18ᵗʰ of March 2018."

Santa started that day by going to the big church on the hill. It had been their family church over the years.

Santa made a huge card with their wedding pictures for everyone to sign. Friends who lived further away could share a message on face book so he could cut and paste it on the card.

After the service in the church, people came down to the reception hall to share the anniversary cake and sign the giant card.

Santa brought the 40 roses that Mrs. Clause was expecting. It was a anniversary tradition to get a rose for each year they had been married.

She was not expecting the card and seemed very delighted that so many people shared their input. It meant a lot to both of them.

The next picture that Santa shared with us was an autumn bouquet that he brought to her for her birthday. Along with it he brought pictures to her of places they had been before to share the autumn colors. This time he had to share them by bringing the pictures to her.

Toward the end of January, Mrs. Claus was able to leave the hospital for about a month. They felt at the time they were on the right track for a possible recovery from this terrible illness.

The last week of February they saw signs of trouble. They new right away what they were and they went back to the hospital quickly. The infection had eaten away at her heart valves. She was having signs of congestive heart failure.

Mrs. Claus had heart surgery and was recovering well. They were both so very happy that they made it together to the 18ᵗʰ of March. Sadly, she took a turn for the worse on the 20ᵗʰ. She was never conscious after that and life support ended on the 22 of March at 1222pm.

At the reception flowers were placed at each table where the guests were seated. At the table where Mrs. Claus usually sat on regular Sunday morning there was an empty vase. The guest shared about their life experiences with Mrs. Claus as they added a flower to the vase.

Santa shared with them how our lives are like an empty vase and beauty comes as friends come along and share their love.

Santa went on to share how he was so ill and soon hospitalized after the memorial services for Mrs. Claus. He lost over 50 pounds in one month. He patted his belly and said.

"It was a good thing for me to lose the 50 pounds, but I do not recommend the C-dif diet for anyone!"

He shared how he ended up in the hospital.

"There was a detour that changed our route home making us drive right by the local hospital." He explained. "As we drove by the hospital my younger grandson spoke up."

"There's the hospital! GO NOW!"

Having met the grandson and observing the relationship between them I could understand this story better.

The next picture we ran across was his middle grandson holding a level and standing on a wheelchair ramp that they had built in the garage. He shared about his grandson who was the same age as Gingerboy. He was an awesome kid who helped him build a wheelchair ramp.

"He seemed to be wired to be a handyman. Like his father who we adopted, he would always be taking things apart to figure out how they work!"

To which I commented to Santa, "You do the same thing, only you do it with people!"

"HO, HO, HO." He stated as he burst into laughter. "You figured that one out pretty good."

"I can tell this is probably Mrs. Claus and your wedding picture, but who is the older couple sitting in front of you?"

"Pop and Grandma!" Santa continued, "They were my mother's parents. They were my inspiration for taking care of kids. They had a large family and still had room in their hearts for more. If I want to talk about living in interesting times, I talk about them. They were born before the first Auto and Wilbur and Orville. They lived to see Buzz walk on the moon."

"Wow!" I replied, "Drastic changes can take place in a lifetime."

We went on to the next picture. It was a picture of Santa sitting on HARLEY.

"That is the outfit I was wearing when I got HARLEY." Santa explained.

He continued, "We had to take all of the medical equipment back to Billings. We also wanted to take a thank you letter to all of the care providers. As we got to the west end of Billings, he (referring to the middle grandson) yelled out.

"There is the HARLEY dealer grandpa! You can go NOW!"

Santa went on to explain.

"So, we did. I went into the dealership and was met by Dutch. I asked him if he had anything that would match my wardrobe. Dutch eyeballed me from head to toe and replied."

"I think I have the perfect ride for you!"

"He brought us over to HARLEY who is black with red pin strips. The pants I was wearing was black with red lace up the side of the legs. HARLEY was a perfect fit except for one thing. The cost was about 3k above what I wanted to spend."

"So, we went around the dealership looking at much of the older inventory. As we did that, I told Dutch about my story with Mrs. Claus and how she recently passed away. My friend and my uncle first turned me on to riding when I was young. When my oldest son was born in May. That summer during the Sturgis Rally, four guys were riding back from the rally. During a hail storm they sought cover on the shoulder of a highway under a bridge. A truck blinded by the storm hit all four of them. Two went to the hospital. One of the two that died that day was a close friend."

Santa continued, "Shortly after that, we were moving out west. We needed cash to make the move. We sold my cycle. After that Mrs. Claus would never let me get another. She would either explain that I had to raise my kids or we could not afford it. Eventually, I just came to tell others that she thought our wedding vows were 'forsake all others including HARLEY-DAVIDSON'.

I broke out in laughter.

Santa replied, "Dutch also laughed and then went on to say that after my loss of Mrs. Claus this would be a good way to go on with life. He was right."

"The rest of the bikes in their inventory were just not suitable." Santa continued. "I kept going back to MY HARLEY. In the mean time Dutch was busy with something. When he came back, I shared that I would come up with the extra 3k to get the right ride and that was this HARLEY."

"As we did all the paperwork." Santa continued, "Dutch shared how the dealership (Beartooth Harley) would always give a free membership to HOG to anyone who bought a brand-new Harley. Dutch went on to say,

"I told your story to the manager. He agreed that coming back to Harley after 40 years also deserves a free HOG membership!"

A tear rolled down Santa's face as he concluded sharing this part of his life.

After he composed himself Santa went on to share how getting back on a Harley was the right choice for him. It gave him a way to go on with life. It helped him meet some very beautiful and caring people. Each time he shared the story about him, HARLEY and Mrs. Claus it touched the heart of others.

"I know!" The story teller replied. "It really touched my heart when you first told it to me!" He said as he wiped another tear from his eyes.

After spending that time with Santa, I could see how this whole story came about. Each picture he has, had a story to go with it. When he first saw a picture of Buddy and me, he did not like the short story that went with it. For Santa, there had to be more to our story than that simple paragraph. Being a diver like us he just had to go much deeper. So now look how many chapters he has written. How one picture and a short paragraph became the story of Buddy and my lives. All from just that one picture and someone who took the time to go a little deeper.

THE LITTLE BROWN CHURCH ON THE HILL

We had to get back home for school for Gingerboy and Cheerleader. Buddy and I went back to the dive shop. We had some classes of new divers to teach for the company.

As a bargaining chip, to let Cheerleader go along with us on the trip, her dad, the Reverend, talked us into coming to his church. Initially, he pressed us to become regular members.

"That's probably never going to happen!" was my first reply.

"At least come and check it out." Was the Reverend's reply

"That I can handle." Was our final agreement.

While there is a huge gulf between members of the gay community and organized religions, many in the gay community have strived and struggled to keep their deep belief in God alive.

"I cannot begin to address those issues." I told the Reverend

He nodded in understanding and went on to say, "Yes, many hateful things have been said by people claiming to be speaking for God. I must confess that I may have said a few myself."

"The church has to decide what it is going to be." I continued. "Does it want to be a country club that has exclusive membership standards. Or does it want to be an emergency room with open doors that will take in anyone with an injured soul?" I asked.

The Reverend asked, "May I use what you just said sometime?"

I concurred.

Now that we were back from the trip, my conscious was bugging me about our agreement. I knew I was going to have to show up at the Reverend's church sometime soon because I was a man who kept his word. For me it was a matter of getting my courage up and just doing it.

Buddy and I often talked about our beliefs. We were pretty similar in our position in this area of our lives. He had not made any agreement with the Reverend and told me,

"You are on your own on this one!"

As I walked up to the church, I thought about Santa again. He had been very supportive of my faith and shared about his struggle as well. We also found that we had common ground in liking that ole song "Little brown church".

Santa shared that they used that song as the entrance hymn for Mrs. Claus's memorial service. Santa went on to share how there really was a little brown church in the vale in Iowa where he was born. He and Mrs. Claus had frequently talked about going to see it but never took the opportunity to do so. Santa indicate that perhaps with HARLEY or with his grandson, this may become a 'bucket list' road trip.

As I approached a little brown church on a hill, I recalled the picture of the little brown church in the vale. It had been many years since I had been inside a church. In spited of the thought of lightening striking me at this point, I took a deep breath and let it all out.

"Just do it." I whispered to myself.

A stranger greeted me at the door and welcomed me.

"I have seen you but we haven't met you before." And she shook my hand. "I have the café down the street from the dive shop." She went on to explain. "I have seen you and your partner several times."

"Small community." I replied.

"Indeed!" she said which brought a big smile to my face.

I settled into a seat toward the back just in case I would need to make a quick escape. At the last minute, Cheerleader snuck in and sat beside me. We quietly gave each other a hug as the service started.

It all start out with a routine that I was familiar with from my childhood days. I thought to myself that not much changed in the church over the years. Everything seemed to go as scripted.

As the Reverend started his sermon, he made a comment that changed all of that.

"I am sorry folks." He started in.

"I have to go with my heart today!" He said as he appeared to throw away his sermon notes.

Earlier he had nodded to me as he noted my presence. With his comment and action, I began to brace myself. Cheerleader reached over and tightly held my hand.

"Recently, I had the pleasure of meeting the fathers of the boy who loves my daughter." The reverend continued.

"He is an awesome boy and I have begun to love him as much as my own son. I sincerely hope that some day he may be my son-in-law If that is God's will and what my daughter wants. That young man had the courage to stand up to me when I was passing judgement on another soul. He challenged my thinking and proved it to be wrong. He proved it to me that I was **wrong**!" He paused for a sip of water.

"In the past, I believed that no child could be raised by parents of the same gender." He continued as cheerleader held my hand even tighter. "I told the boy he was good in spite of the parents he had. The boy corrected me and proved to me that the love his parents have for him is no different than the love I have for my children. That boy also shared how his first parents failed to love him sufficiently. He shared about the devastation he had to deal with as a result of that."

Tears rolled down my face as I thought about the pain Gingerboy, myself and many others all had to deal with when our first parents rejected us in the name of God. Cheerleader pulled out a tissue and wiped my tears.

"He was adopted by fathers who experienced a similar pain." The reverend continued. "Yet they had hearts full of love. Love that their son would need!"

The Reverend continued. "It was then that boy taught me how my hatred of the devil and sin were hurting my chances to reach many souls who need to find a pathway to our God. A forgiving and loving God. A God that taught his fathers well on the proper way to love him. They love him unconditionally just as God has loved us and taught us to love."

I started to notice others with tears as the Reverend continued.

"That boy went on to show me how much love was in his heart. When tormented and teased by others he did not let that pain turn into hatred. He explained how only the devil wins when we let hatred come into our hearts. He challenged me further by pointing out how we sometimes preach selective forgiveness. Each and everyone of us is lost in our sin and will continue to sin until the day we die. We have to stop thinking that anyone is any different than us and needs to be treated with hatred and bigoty."

He paused for a moment, "If there is anyone here who has hatred and prejudice still harboring in your hearts, I want to speak with you now. We love you! God loves you! But there is no room in God's kingdom for hatred. Not even your kind of hatred. And I no longer want to see that kind of hatred in this house of God again. If you feel you must leave you may do so. But know that you will be welcome back when your eyes and hearts have been opened like mine."

The Reverend took a deep sigh and another sip of water before he continued.

He concluded, "My daughter loves that boy. I have no doubt about how much love that boy has in his heart. I am happy that he loves my daughter. His heart is so filled with love that there is even some in there for me! He has asked if someday, when the time is right, if he could become my son-in-law. My reply was that I would be honored!"

My jaw dropped and I turned to Cheerleader who was beaming with a smile that could light up the entire room.

The Reverend was done and the final hymn was sung. Some people quietly walked out the doors of the church. Perhaps they still needed more time think. Perhaps they needed more time with their hatred. But most other came over to congratulate Cheerleader and welcome me back to the church with open arms.

Much later I talked about it with the Reverend and told him they could rename the church.

"The little brown church on the hill?" The reverend replied

"The church with open arms!" I responded

JUST YOUNG DUMB INTENTIONS

They were still in high school when I heard the good news. It was even better when I found out that it was just their intentions to get married someday but not right now. They were still kids falling in love.

Buddy and I needed a long talk with Gingerboy to make sure this was the right life for him.

We first talked about what it meant to be a good father. How each of us had different experiences but all of us had the same need for a loving father.

"The biggest challenge for me in life is to be a better father to you than the one that God gave to me!" I said.

To which Gingerboy replied. "I hope I can live up to that standard! But you and Buddy have set the bar pretty damn high!"

I shared with Gingerboy that I had no doubts that he could meet or beet us. His love was real. It would be sufficient for him to become a good father and a good husband someday.

"But not today!" I emphasized.

A couple days later Gingerboy and Cheerleader came over to our house after a game.

"Dad! We're here." He yelled out as he came into the door. "We got something for you!"

Buddy and I both came to see what they had.

"We found our song!" Cheerleader said

"You gotta listen to it dads!" Gingerboy chimed in

We all sat by the table and listened to the song "**Young dumb broke high school kids**"

As the song ended both Buddy and I applauded loudly.

We turned to each other and shouted, "JINX!"

"Really dads," Gingerboy commented. "I love it when you guys are still kids!"

"Not the 'dumb' part because you're probably smarter than the both of us!" I quickly replied and Buddy nodded with approval to my comment.

"Oh, you guys are a pretty good tag team and would out do me every time you gang up on me!" Gingerboy promptly replied. Buddy then chimed in, "Now don't lose the focus here. This is about the two of you and not the two of us!"

I nodded with what Buddy had to say and comment, "But we have to admit that these kids just did much of our job for us. Oh, there may be a whole lot more talk about this, but hearing this song--you're telling us that you get what we are saying to you. Both of you have some more growing to do."

"We really get that and want this to be right for us!" Cheerleader replied.

Buddy and I also played 'tag team' with the Reverend and his wife. We often called and shared with them what was going on at our place and they also called to share interaction they had had. Some times when I felt lost in this area and they didn't have a good answer either, I got on the cell to my personal mentor on this, Santa.

"How did you and Mrs. Claus hang in there with each other for 40 years?" I asked on my first call.

Santa replied, "That is a simple question that at first I thought I could give you a simple reply. Let me sit down a for this."

"God's will!" is the simple answer. He said before he continued on.

"Having the same mission was the strongest glue that kept us going for so long." He continued

"You especially see it with soldiers. Men who have the same mission with each other form a very tight bond." He continued.

"Buddy and you have that same thing. At first it started out with your diving class. I am sure when you went on dives together it was evident there. Now you have it with the dive shop. You even have it with Gingerboy." Santa replied

"Mrs. Claus and I started out with a similar mission." He continued, "We were in Rochester at the time when we became group home parents. At first, we were just 'young dumb college kids and broke' we were so much in love---Ah" he paused, "let me change that. I am not sure if we were in love or in lust with each other back then. But I asked if she would marry me and she replied that she would. Over the years, as we shared our mission, our love blossomed."

Santa stopped to take a sip of soda, "Where was I, oh ya. Broke college kids needed a job. Mrs. Claus was doing an internship at the time. I was in my last semester of college. I was staying at the same place where she was doing her internship. That place provided free room and board to any college student who would be willing to stay in their dorm and have a probation offender live with them. At the time it was a pretty progressive program that was gaining national recognition. That same organization had a group home for juveniles. There was a vacancy for group home parents. We went thru a rigorous interview for over four hours."

I interjected, "You mean like the one that Buddy and I had to go threw with family services when we adopted Gingerboy?"

"Indeed!" Santa replied as he continued on.

"So, we got the job. Even before we were married and went on our honeymoon, we had the similar mission of raising 9 juvenile delinquent boys."

"Our next mission was the raising of our son." Santa continued. "It just kept going on and on with foster kids, adopted kids, even thru the time we had grandkids."

"Occasionally, we would encounter distractions along the way." Santa continued. "We had to recognize them for what they were and work to get our focus back on what our mission was. Our mission in life."

"Toward the end of the time that Mrs. Claus was with me, our mission changed. Her mission was to fight the disease with all the might that she had. I had to step up to the plate and take care of her. To me, it was interesting how much in those final months our bond and love reignited again." Santa paused.

"I understand how that bond forms from the time when Buddy was in the hospital and rehab center." I chimed in. "Our love for each other deepened more. It surprised both of us how strong our bond to each other became as a result of that. I probably should share this with Buddy." And then my eyes opened even more. "I probably now have a reason to be thankful for that situation with the crew chief. Because of the challenge in our lives we were brought together even more."

"Hate to cut this short, but I have to run and do a favor for a grandson now. I hope I have been of some help for your situation. I hope we can chat some more soon!" Santa closed the conversation.

Before meeting with Gingerboy and Cheerleader, I shared this conversation with Buddy, Reverend and his wife.

"Gingerboy's Santa must be your guardian angels!" commented the Reverend.

MARCH MADNESS

Quarterback's mom called to fill me in on some things that were going on with Santa. She indicated, "He ended up hospitalized for a night and was headed back to Billings Clinic for some follow up care."

"Thanks for filling me in so I will have something to talk with him about!" I indicated to her that we shared an anniversary date and I was planning to call him anyway.

As usual, when I talked with Santa, he tried to keep the focus on me and my family. I filled him in on how our lives for the most part had been pretty routine.

"Gingerboy's Senior football season ended up with the championship. He is now sorting thru some scholarship offers and trying to decide what the best thing will be for him. He has decided on a career like mine in engineering so that eliminated some of the choices." I shared.

"How's buddy doing?" Santa asked

"He just had his physical. He was telling me about the new eye candy at the clinic (meaning the new nurse). He was going on about all that, when he surprised me that the doctor cleared him for diving again." I replied.

"Okay!" I replied. "Enough about us! I hear things about you. So, what's up with you?"

"Who ratted me out?" Santa replied.

"You don't need to know that!" Was my reply.

Santa replied. "Well everyone seems to be making a bigger deal of it than it really is. I shoveled too much show after the first snow storm we had this month. I noticed the changes and went in to get it all checked out. They kept me in overnight to make sure I did not have a heart attack. All the lab work came back fine."

"Well what was it?" I asked

He continued, "They found that my pacemaker was running too fast. It is supposed to keep me about 60 heart rate, so I do not pass out. Something was not right because every once in a while, it would pace at 110 instead. I went up to Billings to get that fixed. They fixed all the electrical system in the heart. Then they also scheduled some tests to check on the 'plumbing' of the heart. It has to be rescheduled because of the storm. I made it up to Billings but the isotope needed for the test was still stuck down here in that 'Arctic Hurricane' that we had."

"Oh ya, I heard about that on the weather channel." I reported. "That was really some storm!"

"Well that wasn't the only storm going on here" Santa continued. "My Grandson rode along to Billings to pick up some things he was going to need. They also sent him along to keep an eye on me. He initially told me that his uncle got into a jam for not taking his medications. When I got back, I got the rest of the story from others."

"Tell me more." I replied

Santa continued. "We could not get back home because the highway home was shut down. At first I thought every highway in the state was shut down because of the storm. The storm really wasn't all that bad north of Piney Creek. The highway from home to here was still open but had to be shut down because of a highspeed chase and potential suicide by cop incident with my grandson's uncle."

"Oh my God! I replied, "What happened?" I asked fearing the worst.

"My grandson's mom got involved as did her other brother who is a police negotiator. They got a three-way call going. Eventually, he came out of his car with one hand on his head and the other talking on the cell phone with the cops." Santa concluded

"Pretty boring there, eh!" I jokingly replied which got him to laughing.

"Okay!" Santa replied, "Anything else going on with you guys?"

"Well ya." I replied.

"Let's have it!" Santa commanded.

"Well after the good news from the doctor, buddy invited me out to celebrate. We took his Silverado and he drove. We were a little way out of town before I asked where we were headed. Buddy just told me we would be there soon." I shared.

I continued, "He put the truck in 4wd and we pulled off the road a little way on a rough dirt drive. He got out and instructed me to follow. We were standing on a knoll that overlooked the city with an awesome view of a small lake with the mountains behind it when buddy asked "Would like to wake up here every morning."

"Oh my!" Santa replied, "You guys are finally doing it?"

"Yep!" I continued, "He bought the land already and construction starts in a couple of weeks!"

A VERY FINE HOUSE

Work on the house was going along well. They were hoping to have it enclosed by fall before the snow started to fly.

Before then, Gingerboy had to decide soon as to which scholarship offer, he was going to accept. He got it down to three options; Texas Tech, South Dakota School of Mines, and University of Alaska. Cheerleader, Buddy and I were all keeping our fingers crossed. We all cheered when he eliminated Texas.

Now it was a choice between a school close to home or a school close to Grandma. Both schools made competitive offers. Both schools had good academic records and the major he wanted. One school was close to our home and the other close to his first home as well as six of his Grandparents.

"Become independent or hang out longer with you guys?" Gingerboy thought out loud.

It was then that Buddy and I proposed our offer. "You can stay here. We have to share the place with you for one year but after that we will be moving to the new house and this place can become your place." It was the offer he could not refuse.

Cheerleader was also going to the same college as Gingerboy. So perhaps the "go with your heart" argument was really the part that sealed the deal.

During the summer he helped around the shop and came along on some of the garbage clean up jobs that the company contracted for. He also studied to get his PADI dive instructor permit. Cheerleader took a job at the local library for the summer that would last into the school year. She was an avid reader and it made sense for her to be around books all day.

By mid-summer Gingerboy talked her into taking a dive and signing up for classes. Our dive shop of course waived any charges for that special student.

"It's a lot of fun." Cheerleader commented, "But I would not want to do it for a living!"

A real highpoint for Gingerboy that summer came in August. Some NFL players had a special football camp that the entire team got to attend. Gingerboy got to snap the ball to an NFL player.

When the NFL player heard about Gingerboy's record of no fumbles on snaps and never missing any block assignment they asked, "Can we take you home with us?"

By mid-October, the outside shell to the house was completed. This was when life really got busy for Buddy and I. We both wanted to put our touch on the place. We subcontracted some of the work for ourselves. So, our weekends and evenings got very busy.

We put in much of the insulation. We hung and taped much of the sheetrock. We hired an electrician who showed us how to string wires properly and supervised us doing some of the electrical work. We made similar arrangements with the plumber. We even helped with some of the tile work.

Sometimes when we were working alone at the house, we could get a little creative with our dress code. Needless to say, our 'dress code' caused some 'construction delays' especially in the evenings. Also, everyone was curious as to how we got the painting done without getting any paint on any of our cloths. Our answer was we just used washable paints.

By late spring much of the interior was being completed. We still had much landscaping and yard work to complete. Especially the drive, which we were frequently getting stuck in. Once the frost was out, we put in a gravel drive with a 30-yard concrete slab by the garage. No one got stuck after that until the blizzard in the winter.

In June, Gingerboy and Cheerleader brought over a house warming gift.

Gingerboy commented, "This gift is bread to warm your house so what better house warming gift could we get for you?"

Goldie (a golden lab) certainly fulfilled all expectations. We now had to remodel the house to include a puppy door and a fenced in area of the yard. While others had to stop and smell the roses Goldie would stop and eat them.

GRANDPA

One evening Gingerboy called and asked if we were both home for the evening. He usually just dropped by unannounced. He indicated he had something to tell us.

When he arrived, he asked, "Would you like to go out on the deck?" where we had a bar. He fixed a drink for each of us. He even gave each of us a cigar and I did not "get it" until he lite one up for himself.

"What's up son?" I asked. "I know you're not a smoker!"

"I will have one with you this time GRANDPAS!" he replied.

"Are you ready for this Gingerboy?" Buddy asked.

"Ready or not here it comes!" was his reply.

I put my arms around him for a big hug and lifted him spinning him around a couple of times.

Gingerboy continued, "Her dad wants us to get married in the little brown church."

"I can understand that." I replied.

"We set a date for three weeks from now. Can you make it?" he asked

Buddy and I promptly replied "Wouldn't miss it for anything!"--"JINX!"

Buddy went on to ask, "Can we have a reception here after the church?"

"We did not think about that. Thanks, that would be really awesome!" Gingerboy replied. "I will have to ask Mrs. Ginger to make sure it is okay!"

"Get used to that!" I replied with a laugh.

"Call her and tell her to get up here now!" Buddy added. "Let's celebrate now!"

"How are her folks doing with this?" I asked.

Gingerboy replied, "They had mixed feelings at first."

"I can understand that, I think we're in that same ballpark!" I replied. "Would they like to come over too?"

"I will give them a call also." Gingerboy replied.

After he was finished with the calls, we all sat down with our cigars.

"How—ahh—ya know what I mean." I stumbled

"It was mostly my fault. I forgot 'trojan man' and we did not have a back up plan." Gingerboy explained.

"So where are we at with school?" I asked

Ginger boy replied, "That would be a good discussion to have when the others arrived. If I stay, I still have to play for the scholarships. It won't be easy but others have done it."

It was the first time that Reverend and MRS R had been to our new house so we offered a tour.

"Oh, heck yes!" MRS R replied. "I have heard so much about it. I was wondering if I would ever get to see it."

"First we have an introduction to make!" Buddy injected. "Can you go get her Gingerboy?"

"Sure thing." He replied.

"Oh, she is so adorable!" MRS R shouted once she saw the puppy.

We offered the Reverend a cigar and he replied, "Oh why not! Give me one Gingerboy."

We thawed some steaks in the micro to throw on the grill. Like pulling a rabbit out of a hat, Cheerleader and MRS R pulled things from the fridge and turned it into a salad.

When everything was ready, I asked the Reverend, "Would you say a prayer for us?"

"Sure!" he replied. "God help us all. Amen!"

I looked at him and said, "That had to be the shortest prayer in your career?"

To which he replied, "And probably the sincerest also!"

Family and close friends were invited to the wedding. I was pleased that ten grandparents were able to come to the event. Four on the bride's side of the family and six on the grooms. The other six included Buddies parents, and both sets of Gingerboy's grandparents. They had stayed in touch, exchanging Christmas and Birthday greetings. This would be their first in person get together since we adopted Gingerboy.

We had to provide some shuttle service for the guest as there was limited parking available at our house for the reception. With a few exceptions the reception guests were limited to family. The house was partially handicap accessible so Quarterback and his mom could stay with us and join the reception. After all, the **BEST MAN**, needed to be at the reception.

The kids also arranged for a dance at the school for the following day. That party was mostly for their friends and by the time of the dance the family quests would be leaving.

Gingerboy introduced us to his grandparents. I was at a loss as to where to go with the conversation. Gingerboy picked up on that and said, "I am such a lucky kid to have so many people who love me!"

The rest of the adults in the room took it from there. The grandparents share about some of the most interesting moments in their lives that they had shared with Gingerboy.

Grandma Lucy started it. "He stayed with me one night when he was younger. When I got up the next day all the frosting on the cake I was bringing to church was gone. He claimed he had nothing to do with it while some of the frosting was still on his face and hair. I just showed him a mirror and he said "oops, I'm busted!"

We all burst out in laughter as we watched Gingerboy's face get as red as his hair.

Quarterback shared about the time they tied Gingerboy up in the closet in hopes that we would leave him behind when we moved.

He went on to say, "When I was deep in despair, this guy was there for me. He is a good man!"

Tears filled the eyes of all the grandparents as Quarterback shared the rest of his story.

Someone said something to the effect that in spite of all the things in his life Gingerboy turned out to be a good man.

It was Gingerboy's time to chime in. "It was because of all those things in my life that I am the man I am today. With the love I got from God and from all of you, I was able to meet every challenge thrown my way!"

I patted him on the back and replied, "I could not have asked for a better son!"

During the wedding reception, I pulled Gingerboy's original grandparents aside for a discussion. Rick and Lucy were parents of his father. Fred and Ethel were his mom's parents. We started out how we all had been raised with similar prejudices regarding sexuality. They shared how they had to set aside those prejudices to love their grandson. Buddy and I shared how we had to set them aside to love ourselves and each other.

I was probing them a little to get an assessment of where things were with Gingerboy's first parents. The grandparents were all pleased to hear that Buddy and I were supportive of rebuilding the bridge between Gingerboy and his biological parents. I shared how we had worked to lay some of the ground work for that.

Adoptive parents, especially of an older child, have to be receptive to the fact that their child is caught in the middle of a situation similar to a child caught between two parents who have divorced. The child struggles with the fact that he has love for both.

Far too often the child gets caught up in a competition between the two. Sometimes the child tries to manipulate that to their advantage by blackmailing one or both parents. While the child may get what they want in that situation they always fail to get what they need. I did not ever want Gingerboy to fail in getting what he needed. After sharing this with all of his grandparents, Lucy and Ethel were cheering me on. The gentlemen were a lot quieter but interested in hearing more.

So, I continued, "I hope someday Gingerboy and his parents are able to rebuild the bridge that broke down."

Rick replied, "That bridge did not break. My son ripped it down!" He continued, "He still has a lot of 'self-pride' to let go of before any bridge can get fixed. We been working on it and so far, not getting much progress."

I asked, "Where's his mom in all this?"

Ethel replied, "Her heart is much more open but she is between a rock and hard place. Losing a son or losing a family. It's tearing her apart!"

Buddy then interjected. "We will be praying for them as well as all of you! Hope God will soften some hearts during all of your lifetimes."

Tears formed in all four of their eyes.

Ethel then asked, "Where is Gingerboy on this issue."

I replied, "He wavers between still feeling the pain and getting angry about it and accepting it and being grateful where he is in life today."

Buddy chimed it, "It is still a struggle for him."

"We can ask Gingerboy just what he feels someday." I indicated, "But not today. Today is time to celebrate and honor this event in his life. It is a challenge that we can continue to work on together."

Gingerboy played well the first year in college, but the team had a mediocre season. The defensive team seemed to be getting run over every time they were on the field. The offensive team just could not keep up.

The blessed event would be in March. The days were getting much longer while the daylight was getting much shorter. We were all busy building the nest. After an ultrasound test, we knew what colors to get for the nursery. Gingerboy and Mrs. Ginger were going to have a Gingerson.

GINGERSON ARRIVES

———————— § ————————

We got a call in the morning from Gingerboy, "It's time!" and the baby arrived 3/22 shortly after noon.

"No need for I D band on that one." Was my reaction to seeing my grandson for the first time.

Gingerboy laughed and replied, "Ya he will be genetically challenged for his whole life!"

Buddy replied, "Were either of you that cute at one time?"

The Reverend and MRS. R were just as proud of their grandson as we were.

I presented our first gift for our grandson.

"I hope it fits soon!" I commented as I realized how small he was.

The first gift was a black motorcycle riding jacket in the smallest size available.

The Reverend burst into laughter.

MRS R. commented, "At least RED and BLACK go well together!"

The second gift came from Buddy. It was scuba gear that could fit a small toddler.

We all broke out in laughter when Mrs. Ginger suggested, "Perhaps he should wear it to his baptism."

"That would be a first and that would be awesome!" the Reverend replied.

"Let's just do it!" MRS. Ginger commented, "let's get it on him to send pictures to all of the greats!"

"Just picture how cool my son will look on his first HARLEY." Gingerboy proudly commented. Tears rolled down his face, "This has got to be the greatest day of my entire life!"

"Tell Ethel to give a picture to my mom!" Gingerboy said to his wife

"I got the right side!" Buddy declared, so I took the left side as both Buddy and I gave Gingerboy and big hug.

Arrangements were made for Gingerson's baptism so invitations could be sent out.

Quarterback was asked and accepted the role of God Parent.

HONEYMOON

"One more baby gift from all 4 of us!" The reverend said as he handed Gingerboy an envelope.

"OH MY GOD!" Gingerboy shouted and quickly added, "Excuse me sir!" as the reverend gave him a stern look.

Gingerboy showed the envelope to his wife and her eyes lit up.

"HAWAII!" She shouted out with glee.

Then a worried look, "But we can't go now. We have a baby to take care of!"

"What do you think grandparents are for?" MRS. R. promptly replied.

The envelope contained an airline ticket and a credit card as well as some cash.

"You have to wait until school is out for the summer!" Buddy chimed in.

"The card has a 3k limit and we will cover it all." I added.

"This isn't fair to you guys!" Gingerboy continued, "We should not have a honeymoon at your expense when you have never been on a honeymoon!"

"We got that one covered." Buddy replied. "You can help watch the dive shop while we go on our honeymoon in May!"

"Can you also watch Goldie?" I asked.

"Not a problem, sir!" replied Gingerboy. "We got it covered!"

Before leaving on our trip the kids got Buddy and I baseball outfits to wear on the trip and to add to our gear collection. We had no trouble figuring out which outfit belonged to who. One jersey had 'pitcher' and the other had 'catcher'.

May in Europe for the older kids for a month!

Our first stop in Europe wasn't your typical tourist destination. We accepted an ole college buddies long standing invitation to come to enjoy some Turkish oil wrestling. It is as popular in Turkey as baseball is in the USA. (the reader is encouraged to look it up on the internet)

We took in more traditional tourist sites in Greece and Italy.

A raucous party in Berlin was impressive but also wore us out. There was so much to do we put in some pretty long days.

It was actually nice and relaxing to get to one of our dive friend's house in the Netherlands to just hang out for a while. He also took us on tour of the Frank house and tulip fields.

A couple of days in London doing tourist stuff and then on to our last stop in Paris.

Fine dining and romantic evenings as well as hitting the tourist sites.

For a couple of gear freaks like us the cherry on top was the time we had at the space camp.

We got to gear up in Astronaut suits and go thru some of the rigorous training and testing they have to experience.

For all of us, it was a dream trip come true. We doubted that the kids would have as much fun as we did. Perhaps we were wrong because they were beaming and looked refreshed when they returned. While us ole farts needed a vacation to recover from our vacation.

BRIDGE REPAIR

§

Gingerson was a couple of years old when we were asked if we could take another trip. The original plans were to go visit Buddies parents and the four greats. Lucy was having some serious health issues and we wanted to assure she had the chance to see her Great-grandson. The plan was for buddy and I to bike down and the kids to fly down. We would meet up at Buddy's mom's place.

We planned the trip to coincide with the Sturgis Rally. We had a grandson in biker gear who needed to see that. Of course, he fit right in because Buddy and I kinda acted his age when it came to things like this. It also was Mrs. Gingers first trip to the rally. She quickly got the hang of the shopping part in down town. With a grandson with us we skipped the bar scene. Buddies step-dad loaned a pick-up to the kids to help haul the gear and grandson along. Buddy and I even swapped with Gingerboy and Mrs. Ginger so they could ride a Harley at the rally. Gingerson only got to sit on the Harley while they were running. He practiced this often with his Papas so he was used to it.

It was then that Gingerboy informed us of a little side trip we were going on. It was time to answer Lucy's prayer. The prayer that a bridge would be repaired in our lifetimes. Gingerboy felt the time was running out for Lucy to see this day.

Gingerboy had also had contact with his biological father without our awareness. They both had agreed to set their difference aside long enough to let Lucy see them together before she was gone. We were going to a family reunion at Pine Island.

It was a comfortable August day in the mountains. A little too hot for us in the basin. The drop in temperature as we drove higher was refreshing.

We stopped off at Steamboat Rock along the way to pay respect to Mrs. Claus. Santa had often talked about this place.

As we were about to leave, Gingerboy commented. "This feels like the time we visited quarterback. I know we need to go do this, but I am clueless on what to say."

"This is strange territory for all of use." I replied.

"Let's just do it!" Buddy chimed in.

When we arrived the four greats came out to great us. I was saddened to see how frail Lucy was looking compared to what she had been like just a couple years ago.

"Still a beautiful lady." I complimented her.

"Since when did you turn into a liar?" she asked then both of us broke into a laugh.

"It really is good to see you again." I commented and she nodded agreement.

"Relax and come on over." Ethel invited us to the picnic shelter. "They haven't arrived yet."

A half hour passed and they still had not arrived. Recalling how promptness was always insisted upon by his first dad, Gingerboy began to worry that he may have had a change of heart.

Finally, a car drove into the lot. As soon as it stopped two teenagers jumped out and were running over to us. They both jumped into the arms of their older brother and almost knocked him over. "Dads, this is my sister and brother." And he introduced us to them.

"Do you want to see my wife and your nephew?" Gingerboy asked

With much exuberance they were off to meet Mrs. Ginger and Gingerson.

Carrying a handful of picnic gear the adults from the car were much less exuberant. Perhaps even subdued.

His mom set what she was carrying down on the ground and gave her son a big hug. His father walked by and put his load on the table.

Gingerboy pick up what his mom had been carrying and brought it to the table.

He introduced us.

"Dads, this is my mom and first dad." Gingerboy seemed to make a point of addressing us all as parents and not by our names.

"Good to get to meet your." I offered my hand to shake.

"Glad to see you." Buddy offered his hand as well.

Dad one without comment shoke each of our hands.

While mom gave each of us a timid hug.

They seemed to linger for a moment.

"Go show'em their grandson." Buddy instructed Gingerboy

"Come on Mom and Dad," Gingerboy said "We may need to rescue him from his uncle and Aunt!"

I thought Gingerboy was being great about addressing them by their relationship and not by their names.

"Oh my God, Look at all that ginger." His dad finally spoke as he saw his grandson for the first time.

"He is so adorable," his mom said.

Then dad one acknowledged a connection between his grandson and buddy and I. "He is even a leather boy too!"

Gingerboy picked up on that, "Yep, he has got a little bit of all his Grandpas."

I just had to smile at how good Gingerboy was doing this.

His mom was taking an instant liking to his wife as most people do.

We all seemed to be on our best behaviors as the picnic dinner got under way. But we all seemed to be on edge waiting for the next shoe to drop. Waiting for someone to misstep.

As the afternoon progressed, they began to relax. They were having a good time with each other.

While I was glad to see all of this take place, I also felt a little left out.

When Gingerson came running over to me I made the first misstep.

"Oh, you finally going to give ole grandpa some time?"

"Remember what you taught me dad! Jealousy and envy just make you look a lot smaller!" Gingerboy said.

Dad one then chuckled.

"What are you laughing about." I snapped

"I see he gives as much crap to you as he gave me!" Dad one replied as he patted me on the back.

"Ya, He always was quiet a boy and now, thanks to all of us, he is a man we can all be proud of!" I replied shaking dad one's hand with one hand and embracing Gingerboy with the other. Buddy and dad one joined in the embrace of Gingerboy as the rest of the group applauded.

Lucy sat at the table with tears in her eyes. Tears of joy that this took place in her lifetime. A few weeks later she was no longer with us. A week after his mother had passed away, Dad one called buddy and I.

"I want to thank you for that special day." He continued, "It meant so much for my mom. I am not sure where things will go from here between the three of us, but I do want you to know I did appreciate what you did for my mom."

"One more thing." He then added, "I think you guys did a good a job finishing what I had started. I really screwed up and let my hate for guys like you get in the way of loving my son."

I replied, "At one time I was a son like your son. All son's need to be loved by their dad. Let's hope we did our jobs well enough that our grandson has a better father than we were.

FAREWELL

At four years old, Gingerson was full of joy and curiosity. His joy filled the heart of everyone who knew him. He was the center of his father's universe. If that sharp wit was not a genetic characteristic, he sure learned it well from his father. He loved spending time with his two grandmas and four grandpas. His mom was his favorite sweetheart and he loved his father with all of his soul. His mom taught him how to cheer the loudest for his father when he was on the football field.

His father, Gingerboy had graduated the previous year from engineering school. His football career was an unblemished record of never fumbling a snap or missing a block.

He was starting his career as an Aqua Engineer similar to what his dads did for a living. Like his dads he was a regular gear freak. He loved to gear up anytime he could. He and his first dad were steadily repairing the bridge that they had broken. In spite of the distance between them in many different ways they still valued their love for each other.

Mrs. Ginger was still his greatest cheerleader. She knew she could not compete with his love for gear, Harley and other kinky things. She understood she did not need to compete for his love of anything or anyone. She understood his need for unconditional love. That was the bond that held them together as well as their love for their child.

While making many new friends along the way he still had a special friendship with Quarterback. He was a trusted life long friend. No mater how kinky or twisted their minds could get they willingly heard each other out and tried to help each other on life's journey.

His relationship with Buddy and I remained sound. He was our son and yet at times he was our mentor. He could open our hearts and minds in ways that no others were able to.

There was no warning. On his son's fourth birthday he was heading for home when there was a sudden jolt in the earth. Buddy and I just left the shop when the jolt hit. It knocked us to the ground just as we were about to get into the pick-up. We were fortunate to be outside the shop as a portion of the building collapsed. We scrambled to rescue others from the debris. The scream of sirens soon filled the air. It seemed like they were everywhere.

Once we were assured our coworkers were okay or their minor wounds mended Their attention and ours turned to others and our thoughts to our families. Either the power to the towers was knock out or the cell lines were all jammed as everyone in the area was trying to do the very thing we were doing. Trying to get in touch with loved ones.

We were ten blocks away from the daycare where Gingerson attended. Except for a few broken windows the building was mostly intact. We were somewhat relived but would not feel certain until we found our grandson. When he emerged with only a minor scratch next to his right eye, we were over joyed. His mom soon joined us. She had a harder struggle through more debris to get there than we had encountered. Their home was no longer suitable for shelter as a wall was missing.

Her concerns quickly changed to her parents and her husband. We encouraged her to head for her parents place first. We hoped they were in a safe location where we could all seek shelter. A location we could use as a meeting place. We had no clue as to where Gingerboy could be. We left a note where it could be easily found.

We arrived at her parents place and found it to be mostly untouched. The Little brown church was being opened as a shelter for any in need of a refuge. We went about the business of helping in what ever way possible. Hoping that our son was okay and doing the same thing we were doing.

Fires began to break out in various parts of the city. Fighting the fires became a problem because of the broken water lines. There was no water at the Reverends place either. We left notes so people could find us. We hoped our place was intact and that it had sufficient water from our separate system. The problem would be of getting to it thru all of the rubble along the way. The going would have to be slow as there were large gaps in the ground.

As if things were not bad enough already the tremble of after shocks began. Some of them felt as strong as the initial shoke. Out of fear of more damage to weakened structures people would shy away from the buildings.

We started to make our way thru the debris to our place. We had to figure out alternatives to get around damage areas. It would take us the rest of the day to get there. Just beyond our place the road was no longer passable. We had a single complicated route in and out.

Our place was untouched and the water was working. We were happy we had placed our own solar panels and batteries to provide power for the water pumps. Mrs. Ginger, Mrs. R. and Gingerson would be safe here. The Reverend, Buddy and I went out to see if we could be of help to others. We loaded chain saws into the truck and got out the tractor with front end loader to help move debris. Smoke from all the fires was filling the air. Before it got dark, we returned to the house. We tried the phones again to no avail.

We could get news over the satellite and the emergency broadcast network. The main quack was 9.8 and after shock were as high a 6.8. Fires were out of control but fortunately a light rain began that helped suppress the fires. Reports were that the hospitals were overwhelmed with injuries but so far, the casualty count remained low. Hundreds were still unaccounted for. The airport was being restored as quickly as possible to help fly in needed aid.

As the power got restored the cell service began working again. Buddy received a call from the nurse who had taken care of him when he was in the hospital.

"I think this is your son here. We have no positive ID on him but I remember the Ginger hair. Can you try to make it down here?"

"We're on our way!" Buddy replied

Buddy explained who it was that called. Reverend and MRS. R. said they would stay at our place with Gingerson until we returned or called if possible. Picking our way to the hospital took a couple hours. It was Gingerboy.

The next day they explained how grave the situation was. We prepared for the worst but still prayed for the best. It would take 24 hours to know for certain what we were dealing with. We stayed by his side. The nurse told use both the positive and negative signs to look for. We only saw the negative signs over the next 24 hours.

We let Quarterback and the rest of the family know what the situation was.

Buddy cried as he recalled what it was like to be four years old and say goodbye to his daddy for the very last time.

I cried as I thought of all the joy he had brought into the world and how very much it would be missed by me.

We had to do what Gingerboy would have wanted us to do. We had to say goodbye and trust God until we met again in heaven.

THAT'S A WRAP

Like the intermission, we invited you all here today to wrap up any loose ends that are hanging out there. Perhaps also the author will leave some loose ends to get the readers minds racing off to their own conclusions. After all this story all started when he saw that picture of Buddy and I. The author just let his mind run wild with it and look what became of all of us!

There were many nights when the sun set while he was on the computer writing about our lives. There were even some nights that the sun rose again and he was still there at the computer. He wrote this book during the winter. During times when the snow was flying or it was just to damn cold to ride his Harley. He was approaching the anniversary of the passing of his love for 40 years. We got him to focus on the lives of the various characters in this book so he would not slip into any self-pity. So far it seems to be working. But he confided in me that he worries that he may slip into our fantasy world too far. So far, he hasn't done that yet.

He also struggled with me about letting others read this story. Initially I talked him into just sharing with those who he felt could handle it. He started out by sharing small, safe, pieces of it. Pieces that they could easily swallow without chocking on. Then he was ready for the next step. To share the whole thing with someone who he trusted. You know the people. The ones he loves and trusts to be honest about it and not get too uptight over what he had to write.

He was worried that some readers may throw the baby out with the bath water. He thought some of the stuff included might be to spicy for the pallets of some readers.

He pointed out to me that "Some of the bedroom scenes with buddy and me were too hot for some people to handle yet."

To which I replied, "Some of the readers may throw the whole book out and call it trash just because buddy and I love each other." I then thanked him for keeping our romance hot and passionate. "They will hate to admit it but those hot juicy parts may be just what they needed to keep it interesting."

"I gotta go now to get my grandson off to school!" The author commented. "Story teller, Thanks for staying up all night with me! Tell the others how much I appreciate them helping me get thru this difficult time in my life! All of you loved me and helped me know I was loved and helped me stay on my life highway!" He concluded, "Story teller, can you handle it from here!"

"Sure, SANTA!" I replied as he ran off to another real day in his life. He returned a few minutes later to report that his grandson was sick and he would have to tend to him. He was also grounded from his Harley because of some issues with his pacemaker that he promised his daughter he would resolve before riding again.

"She is getting to be more and more like her mom." Santa commented.

He really needed some sleep now any way. But I knew from time to time he would be back at the computer again with all of us.

The rest of us will go on with our lives.

As for the author, he hopes that there may still be many chapters still left in his life. God's not finished with him just yet. A piece of each character may be a part of his life. Or he may be a part of each character. You may never be able to figure out who he really is by reading this book. He confided in me that he wanted to keep everyone guessing. He is the kind of guy who can be sensitive to what his friends say and think about him. Yet again, if you try to impose your hatred or bigoted views on him, he may be just like me and will tell you to "Go fuck yourself" as he mounts his Harley and rides off into a sunset.

BE CAREFUL WHAT YOU PRAY FOR

The story continues, as young men we signed up for the human droid program in order to become divers. At the time we were fully on board with giving up our lives if necessary, to meet the needs of the mission.

Being gay, bi or straight is not a big deal to any droids. It was all about the gear that turned us on. Being in heavy diver gear 24/7 gives immense pleasure to the droid. Before his assimilation, the droid never imagined that he could experience this level of happiness. Diving, living in controlled environment, wearing the equipment feels so good, this is why real gear men seek the ultimate opportunity to be total gear freaks.

Other divers, just like us, willingly signed away their lives just to be geared up as much as possible. The pleasure of being geared up was very addictive. It pushed all the buttons in our pleasure centers and pumped adrenaline throughout our human bodies. To us it seemed like a dream come true. Nothing could be better than being encapsulated in the gear. To be doing what we loved to do and getting paid to do it. Like pro football players we would do this until our human bodies wore out.

Many of us started out with interest in other gear. For Buddy it was biker gear that got him started. The leathers for street biking and the motocross gear for the dirt. Racing suits for the speed track and street racing. The snug fitting helmets and the boots. At first, he thought he was using the gear as a way to grow out of his desire for diapers. What actually happened was a desire to have both at the same time. He liked the 'black and white' look of chaps and diapers.

My first gear addiction got started with the sports gear. First with football gear and then hockey gear. The well-padded thighs and hips. The head gear down to the cup held snug in place all drove me nuts. Tie me up in gear with no chance of escape and I was in heaven. Buddy would throw a diaper on me and I was set for the weekend.

Then we met up with the diving gear. The ultimate gear experience was the dry suits that took us out of the regular environment and encased us in the gear. I dreamed of even higher addiction of becoming an astronaut. But at the time that club was very elusive and beyond my reach.

We all looked forward to completing the transformation. That time when we were no longer human. The time when we could be permanently encased in our gear. There was no place we couldn't go encased in our gear. We liked to play in the mud in our back yard. In our gear we could be totally immersed in the mud. During the training sessions, astro-droid recruits often ejaculate inside the space suit. The orgasms were so intensive that two diver technicians must hold the droid from falling over.

A total gear freak that I met on line once told me, "If it excites you and scars the crap out of you at the same time, it probably means you should do it!"

Sometimes the biggest fear I had was that I would like something too much and not be able to get enough to satisfy my desires.

There are some who felt the need to be doped up on drugs or booze in order to get thru life. To me they were missing out on life. They were numbing themselves to the feelings and to the experience they were having.

I, on the other hand, wanted to experience life to the fullest. Even if any given experience wasn't the most pleasant thing, I still wanted to feel it. I was hooked on reality as well as all the gear that went with it.

"At least I am not strung out on drugs" Would always be a good excuse for me to get into some more gear. Even when I mixed a variety of gear, I had no fear of an overdose.

A friend once said it best, "There was only one thing that kept us human. Diving is not only about going underwater. Diving is a team sport. It's about friendship, learning to take care of each other. Adjusting your buddy's mask and other gear to assure a good fit. Making sure that he will be safe during the dive."

I believe that this is the most beautiful aspect of diving--such close friendship that you can trust putting your life in your buddy's hands. When you are surrounded by sharks you got each other's backs.

With much of the gear, we all started out in solitude. We thought we were the only one in the world who would have a hard on for gear. Some gear freaks out there are still alone in their little closets. For most of us the isolation was depressing and we somehow managed to crack open our closet doors and find others out there who shared our same desires. Yes, many of us gear freaks would love the comfort of being encased in the safety of gear for the remainder of our lives.

But we all would shed our gear and expose our self to the reality of our world to take care of the ones we love. A relationship with another person is always more important than any relationship with gear.

I do have some directions for those who would ridicule or torment us for who we are. Please take very good aim when you target us. None of us would want your 'shit' to splatter onto those close to us who we love the most. I hope you can agree that they do not deserve it.

When I told Santa about my prayer to be encased in gear he just broke out in laughter.

"When I was a young man I was teased about my curly hair." Santa continued, "I prayed that my curly hair would go away. My prayer got answered." He lifted his wig and pointed to his bald head. "Always be careful about what you pray for!"

THE SEQUEL

§

Gingerboy had a living will that indicated he had signed up to donate his body to the human droid program. The program was in its infancy stages at the time he had signed up. He would be the second one from our state to be in the program. The program would take those humans who no longer had upper brain activities. They were legally brain dead.

Life support would remain on as the process began. While the upper brain was dead, it would be vital to save as much of the remaining tissue as possible for a good functional droid.

First and foremost, the family of the victim would be given time to let go and start the grieving process. Their loved one had passed away. If they were a religious family, like we had become, the Chaplin or the family minister would be involved at this point. The Reverend recognized the hospital Chaplin and introduced him to us. The last rights had already been spoken.

The program had decided at this stage in its development that it would be best if minor children say their farewells in the traditional manor. We had provided Gingerson that opportunity already.

The program was evolving and now would allow a small number of family members to stay and witness the process. The Reverend, Buddy and I were the only ones who requested to remain. We all had to attend a class that explained to us what the process entailed. We were warned to not freak out. That while the body may respond and appear alive, it was no longer our son. It was now a humanoid droid. The droid would not have any of our son's memory. Our son was officially pronounced dead.

As all of the other family members left the three of us remained. The team of specialist came into the room and asked, "Are you folks all ready for this now?"

"Ya" Buddy replied.

"Let's just do it!" was my reply.

The Reverend just nodded his head.

A gurney was brought into the room. Gingerboy's body was moved to the gurney. All of the iv's still remained. While he still had a heartbeat, he had been pronounced dead due to lack of brain activity. Even the law of our state had been altered to recognize death as the cessation of brain activity.

Only one of us could ride along in the van with Gingerboy to the rehab center where this process would continue. Buddy drew the straw to go with Gingerboy's body. The rest of us would have to ride in a separate vehicle. At the center his body was placed in a special suit. The body would be fastened securely to prevent any damage during the process. Once in the suit the body was moved to a sling.

"It is best to use a sling as it will move with the body as needed."

"There can be much convulsing as we proceed" One of the technicians reminded us of what they had said in the class.

They did some last-minute identification processes to assure they had the right body.

"We are set!" One of the staff members yelled out.

"Are you folks sure you are ready for this?" He looked toward us.

"Let's do it!" Buddy and I chimed in together and the Reverend nodded.

An attendant remained with us throughout this entire process to assure our welfare.

He assured we remained well hydrated and had snacks for us. They did not need us passing out on them.

As they proceeded, they explained each step along the way.

"These injections will cause a lot of convulsing. It will seem as if he is in a lot of pain. But previous participants have not reported awareness of pain at the time of completion." He explained.

As the injection went in the body began to react. At first it was just minor movement but as the injection progressed, they became very violent.

"I hope they are right about him not feeling any of this." I whispered to Buddy. "I would not want to put anyone thru this if they knew what was happening to them."

Due to sterile surgical requirements we had to be in a separate observation room for the second step of the process. In the class we were instructed that this is where the artificial intelligence units are placed into the droid.

While the droid was still in the restraining suit for safety reasons, this part of the process was much less active. Occasionally, there would be a slight twitch or movement as different parts of the body were connected to the new intelligence center. The intelligence center was about the size of a thumb. Any old brain tissue would decay and had to be removed.

"We try to retain as much as possible of the previous brain that is still functioning, but we have to make sure we remove all the dead tissue." The surgeon explained over the intercom.

This surgeon was not from around here, but for some reason he seemed familiar to me. I thought I had seen him somewhere before. If not him it must have been someone very similar to him. Having the mask on disguised much of his face. We had been told he was an outside specialist that came in for this procedure.

Finally, after 12 hours, the procedure was completed.

"The droid will be going to a rehab center for several months while the programing processes continues." We were told by the surgeon.

He continued, "I will be dropping in from time to time to check on the progress he makes. The droid may retain some of your son's characteristics but his brain was dead and had to be removed. The damage was very extensive. It was far worse than what we had to work with for you Buddy."

The surgeon went on to explain how the same technology had been used in Buddy's recovery. He was the first to use it in this state. At that time buddy had not been declared dead. He still retained some of his memory. The technology was used to supplement in areas that had been damaged.

It was then that I recognized who surgeon was. He had been buddy's surgeon when buddy was in rehab. I began to put the pieces together.

"Have I been living with a droid all these years?" I asked.

"Yes, Buddy was number one up here!" the surgeon replied.

Buddy was as surprised by this news as I was.

THE FINAL CHAPTER OF BOOK ONE

While this is the final chapter for the characters of this book, You the readers of this book are not done yet. Hopefully what was written here hasn't put any road blocks in your way. Hopefully some of what was written here can be an inspiration and help for all of you.

May your hearts be filled with love and may you share that love with others. Even if they are strangers to you now. Especially if they are someone you already love.

Now you go on to the next chapters in your lives. When your time comes to write the final chapters I hope you are as happy and fulfilled by your life as I have been.

Always live your life like it is an open book because there is always someone reading it or reading more into it.